Pol Koutsakis was born in 1974 in Chania, Crete, Greece. He is a playwright, novelist, and screenwriter. In 2007 he won the National Award for Playwriting in Greece. His plays have been staged in the USA and the UK and published in Canada. He is currently living in Perth, Australia, with his wife, daughter, and son. *Athenian Blues* is his first crime novel and the first of his books to be translated into English. The next in the series, *Baby Blue*, will be published by Bitter Lemon Press in 2018.

www.polkoutsakis.com

ATHENIAN BLUES

Pol Koutsakis

BITTER LEMON PRESS
LONDON

BITTER LEMON PRESS
First published in the United Kingdom in 2017 by
Bitter Lemon Press, 47 Wilmington Square, London WC1X 0ET

www.bitterlemonpress.com

First published in Greek as *Ιερά Οδός Μπλουζ*,
Patakis Publications, Athens, 2010 © Pol Koutsakis, 2010

English translation © Pol Koutsakis, 2017

The moral rights of Pol Koutsakis have been asserted in
accordance with the Copyright, Designs and Patents Act 1988

A CIP record for this book is available from the British Library

ISBN 978–1–908524–76–8
eBook ISBN: 978–1–908524–77–5

Typeset by Tetragon, London
Printed and bound by CPI Group (UK) Ltd, Croydon, CR0 4YY

For Nano, Despina and Athina.
Three generations of love.

1

A few of them were kicking and screaming, but most of the immigrants followed orders, as the police shoved them out of the building. They didn't seem to understand they were being told that the abandoned block would soon collapse.

I kept walking on the other side of Sacred Way Street, to a place that supposedly offered the best food in town. The purplish complexions of the diners were a fine contrast to the pinched faces clustering around the Médecins du Monde truck, waiting for handouts. I was early, but I could wait.

When you're invited by a client who foots the bill, you go. Especially when the client is a stunning redhead, about five feet nine, with curves other women pay a fortune to acquire and eyes like the sea. I'd seen her plenty of times on magazine covers and wondered how much make-up they'd plastered on her and how many hours had been spent to Photoshop that look. Now that I had the original right in front of me, though, I tended to think that her photos didn't do her justice.

"You must be Mr Stratos Gazis," she said when she finally arrived, holding out her hand. Husky voice, erotic. It had been years since anyone called me "Mr…"

Stratos Gazis is my real name. I don't have any problem using it for my work because officially Stratos Gazis has been dead for years. Burnt to ashes in the house where he lived alone, leaving nothing to identify him by, which is why the police closed the case. You don't need to know the name on my passport and ID card. For your own good.

"Just call me Stratos," I said, shaking her hand.

"And I'm just Aliki."

She flashed me a girly smile, and sat down on the velvet-covered chair opposite. She was over thirty but looked ten years younger. Opening her tiny black handbag on which the maker's name was written in huge gold letters, she caught my glance.

"Kitsch, I know. But since they pay me to show off their products…"

She slipped her hand into the bag – long, slender fingers – and took out a pack of Marlboro Reds.

"Doesn't bother you, eh?" she said, holding it up. "I've booked us a smoking table, I can't rid myself of the devils."

By way of reply I took out my lighter.

"Perfect," she murmured, as she bent over the flame and fixed her gaze on me, appraisingly. As if estimating how deeply she was getting in trouble. Or how much more trouble than she already had.

"Before we start, shall we order something to drink? – And eat, of course. I haven't had a bite all day and I'm not one of those always-on-a-diet girls; when I'm hungry I just can't function."

She waved those long fingers. "They look after you here – they're used to VIPs and all that rubbish."

So sweet, so calm, so natural... I'd nearly forgotten that she had invited me there to discuss how I would kill her husband.

My mother always told me that you could trust people with long fingers. It's the stubby-fingered ones you have to watch.

Mum. How convincing you made everything sound. Even utter bollocks.

2

Teri had phoned me two days earlier, on the number known only by the three people who would protect me with their lives, if necessary. It was dusk and I was wandering down Adrianou Street, where many shops hadn't dared to open, twenty-four hours after the biggest riots of the past six years. Some of the burnt Greek flags and rubbish bins had still not been collected from the surrounding streets in Plaka, and the broken ATMs and shopfronts would take days if not weeks to repair. I ducked into "Everything & More", the greatest shop for collectors of old magazines. Thomas, a sixty-year-old Greek–Australian, who still had blond streaks, had been trying to sell it for the past three years, but who was buying? I'd happened to be in his shop, looking for a magazine I'd loved as a kid, when the private bailiffs arrived, sent by the bank to which he owed thirty grand. Neither the bailiffs nor the bank have bothered Thomas since. And I am allowed to take any magazine I like for free. I had just said hello to Thomas, who was sitting in a black armchair smoking his pipe, when my phone rang.

"Good evening," said Teri, before I'd even opened my mouth.

"Hi," I said.

After she'd had the operation, I would often add "man" at the end of my greeting. Depending on her mood she would slam down the receiver or swear at me. Teri's too proud of her new sex to put up with any crap. The first and only time after the change that I called her by her old name, "Lefteri", she hit me with an uppercut that would have made any boxer jealous. If she weren't five feet five and 130 pounds, while I am six feet three and the scales show me hovering just over 220, she'd have probably knocked me out. She operates only by appointment and mostly in hotels, so I'm less worried about her – or about any customer who rubs her up the wrong way. Back then, I trailed round the streets in the small hours to check that she was OK. The other girls jumped to the conclusion that I was her pimp – it was no use trying to explain we'd been close friends since our schooldays. And Teri doesn't do explanations anyway.

"Boy, do I have a big one for you. Do you know Aliki Stylianou?" she asked.

"The model? Even I've heard of her."

"Wow," she said. "Seven whole words. What's with the verbal diarrhoea?"

"Just get on with it."

"She's not only a model. Lately she's also been doing a bit of acting."

"Good for her."

"She wants to have a word."

"How come?"

"She's got a problem. She had a heart-to-heart with her best friend, who happens to be a friend of mine. And the best friend contacted me – for some reason people think that if you're a whore you must have connections with caretakers like you."

"Which you do."

"When I was a beautician did she ever ask me the best way to bump someone off? I thought of giving her a piece of my mind but Stylianou's loaded and I didn't want you to miss the chance. So when the friend asked me to make discreet enquiries, I swallowed my pride and said I would."

"What's her problem?"

"She's got one more husband than she needs."

"You mean, two?"

"I mean one. She wants a clean slate."

Being a caretaker is my job. I take care of things that are only talked about in whispers. That very few can undertake. Things that people are willing to pay handsomely to get done, without wanting to know any details. Afterwards, they want to try and wipe their memories clean. I don't know if they ever manage but, as far as the business is concerned, I'm their man.

3

"Let me make something clear," I said.

"Yes?"

Aliki tossed back her head and smoothed her hair with her hand. She had a very long, very white neck. A swan. A picture flashed into my mind of her slowly curving it back while someone kissed it. I tried to concentrate.

"The fact that I'm here doesn't mean that I've agreed to do any job."

Another speech. Fourteen words. Teri would be proud of me.

"I understand. You told me on the telephone, and your... friend... explained."

"I'm thinking of saying no."

"Did I do something to annoy you?" she asked, in an even huskier voice than before, leaning towards me across the table, her hands folded, fixing her eyes on mine. Teri, who is crazy about surveys and statistics, told me that in a poll to find the most desirable woman in Greece, Aliki Stylianou got seventy-five per cent of the vote – three out of four Greek men wanted her. The fourth man probably voted against her just to be awkward.

"You've already broken two of my rules even before we met."

"My lateness, you mean. I know. Sorry, but the director wouldn't let me go. It was the final scene; I'd have put back the whole production if I hadn't stayed. Already a lot of the actors are looking down on me, being a model and all – especially the women – and I didn't want to make things worse. So few series are given the green light, I was lucky even to get the part. Could I have some more wine?"

I had ordered an expensive Californian Chardonnay. It had a bitter-sweet taste, as if it couldn't make up its mind what it wanted to be. Aliki had already downed the first glass. I poured her another.

"Yassou," she said.

I nodded. We drank in silence. Aliki appeared to be enjoying it so much she closed her eyes. A drop of wine was hanging from her top lip. I found myself waiting for her tongue to lick it away.

"Hot in here, isn't it?" she said.

She stood up and slipped off her jacket, revealing a tight, short-sleeved blouse. All the men in the restaurant looked at her, more or less discreetly.

"And my second sin?" she said, smiling, as she sat again.

"I suggested meeting somewhere quiet. You insisted on coming here. Where the smart set hang out."

Despite the economic crisis you still needed to be well connected to get a table here.

"It's the only place where we can speak freely without being bothered by anyone."

"That's what you said on the phone."

"The way my life is, the only place to be invisible is in a crowd."

Suddenly she turned serious. No trace of a smile, no tossing head or searching tongue. I could have sworn that I saw a tiny wrinkle appear briefly on her forehead. I like it when the person opposite you suddenly appears totally genuine. Unfortunately, this usually happens only at the end of a job, when the person opposite realizes that in a few seconds it will all be over.

"You know what would have happened if we had gone to some little hideaway? Someone would have secretly papped us and tomorrow morning you'd have been plastered all over the tabloids as my latest lover. And my husband would have got hold of the same photographs through the creeps he has shadowing me – two I've noticed, but there could be more – and then he'd thrash me, once again. Yassou."

I think it was that line she used as she raised her glass that hooked me. It takes a lot of guts to say "Yassou" right after "he'd thrash me, once again". I still wasn't entirely sure she was sincere, of course. And I have to be sure to undertake a job. There's a reason for that. The reason is that everybody is trying to find a way to feel good about themselves. At the end of the day, whatever you've been up to, you have to find the trick. Throw the switch. Have nothing to niggle your conscience. Which is why public hospital surgeons occasionally do operations without the incitement of a bribe, why politicians once in a while help people without expecting a reward and priests sometimes take something from the collection tray to give to the poor.

To throw the switch.

My way is simple. My potential employers have to give me a good reason why the proposed target deserves to be hit. And what they say needs to be confirmed by my own research. The type and difficulty of the hit is not important. It doesn't even matter if I find the employer likeable or repugnant – people who hire me aren't exactly angels, anyway, even though Aliki Stylianou seemed to come close. If my clients were the good guys, they wouldn't be my clients. And if I expected to find real ladies and gents to pay me to kill I'd have to find another profession – which would be a pity because I really excel at what I do.

I need to be persuaded. And to know that the employer can cover my fee, of course. I am a caretaker with a conscience. A fine thing, the human conscience. It forgets. It adapts.

"Explain 'once again'."

"Does it really need explaining?"

"It does."

"Vassilis is jealous. Pathologically. Paranoically. Since the first day we met. Whenever he scents danger he… erupts."

"And you're the victim?"

"Not at first. All that started a few months after the wedding."

"And you've been married…?"

"Nearly three years. Been in hospital twice with fractures. He only hits me on the body, so that he can palm off my injuries as some kind of accident. We're always changing doctors to avoid detection."

Unconsciously, I glanced down at her when she mentioned her body. I quickly raised my eyes, but not quickly enough to avoid her notice.

"I can show you some scars and bruises if you don't believe me…"

Cigarette smoke wrapped her in a cloud much lighter than her expression.

"Doesn't anyone suspect anything?"

"I don't think so. But even if it's crossed their mind, they simply dismiss it. Everyone who knows Vassilis doesn't simply love him, they *adore* him. You don't hear a bad word about him. A journalist called him the 'guy without enemies'."

"He obviously didn't ask your opinion."

She granted me a half-smile and took a gulp of wine. Each swallow drained a quarter of the glass. At that rate we'd get through three bottles that evening. It didn't matter. She was paying.

4

I'm not the most talented person in my profession. I'm sure of that. I'm not the fastest draw, nor much of a street fighter, and though I know a few martial arts moves, no way am I an expert. But if I'm not the most talented, I'm the best. The reason is my passion for method, which I owe to one of the only two theatrical performances I've ever been to.

A large part of my life has been spent in cinemas, watching film noir in particular. I know most of the classics off by heart: it's the only kind of art I like. The only one that bears any relation to real life. I was as indifferent to the theatre as I was enthusiastic about the cinema. The big attraction of plays being live meant nothing to me. My mum's view was: "It's not for the likes of us, my boy, but for educated people who understand art." But one summer, her cousin persuaded her to go to a show, and she took me with her. What put me off was the sense of risk; how, at any moment things might go wrong. An actor might mess up his lines, or forget them completely. The sound could go wrong, or the lights fail. When I pay to see art I want to escape risk. I want to escape from life. Life is full of imperfections. If art doesn't surpass life, what use is it to me? Which is why, when I pay to see art, I go to the movies.

Then I met Chryssoula. She was eighteen, two years older than me, and a member of an amateur theatre group. I looked older than I was. She kept nagging me to go to rehearsals with her. I didn't especially care for her, but I did fancy her, so I went to the dress rehearsal. The cast had put whatever they could beg, borrow or steal into a production of *Hamlet*. I had no idea what it was about. Chryssoula told me she was playing Ophelia. Chryssoula, Ophelia, who cared? After all, how much worse could it be than the televised stagings of *Monday Night Theatre* I had tried to watch a couple of times at home, before falling asleep in the armchair? But it was. Chryssoula's talent was for being beautiful, not acting. She delivered her lines with all the conviction of a failed politician. And her performance was the best of the lot. Ophelia's drowning was a deliverance. Before that, however, the freckly kid playing Polonius, Ophelia's father, had managed to say: "Though this be madness, yet there's method in it." *Method*. I didn't know then how famous the line was. I only knew that I felt as if Freckles had taken a knife and carved the word in my mind. *Method*. I didn't yet know exactly what I wanted to do, but that evening I became convinced that, as long as I did it with *method*, I would succeed.

Method, in my line of business, means research. Whoever has all the information at their fingertips always has the upper hand. First, I gather information about the new client. For someone to find me they have to be recommended by someone I trust – I've made enough money to be able to pick and choose. The luxury the rich enjoy. I check out the client, and if I don't like what I find, they never get to meet me. When I do take someone on, by the time of our first meeting I'll probably know more about them and their target than they do themselves.

With Aliki's husband, little digging was necessary. Vassilis Stathopoulos was one of the most well-known and best-loved men in Greece. The invincible lawyer. The defence attorney who had featured in all the big trials over the last ten years, and succeeded every time in getting people off who seemed to have no chance. He had earned enormous sums in compensation for men and women fired by global corporations. He had proven the innocence of people who everyone believed to be guilty. He had taken the Greek State to the European Court of Human Rights over its treatment of thirty illegal immigrants and won, against a team of the best lawyers in Athens. Then he took the government to the Supreme Administrative Court over the salary cuts of soldiers, police officers and pensioners, and got the law overturned. His clients were often seen to hug, kiss him and hoist him on their shoulders like a football hero. The secret of his success? A bit like mine, as he explained in an interview: he only took on people he felt worthy of his talents.

Not one bad word had been said about him in any of the newspapers, not even the tabloids. He wasn't just "the man without enemies", he was the "guardian of the poor", the "angel of the underprivileged". Journalists ran out of superlatives to describe him.

According to another poll – Teri, again – forty per cent of Greek mothers would choose Vassilis as the ideal partner for their daughters. Forty per cent. Greece's most desirable bachelor, before he married Aliki. He didn't get the percentage of popular vote that his wife did, but he had managed something more important. We all like to see a celebrity make an arse of themselves but he remained someone everybody admired. So Aliki had to persuade me that he was, in fact, a monster. That their smiling photographs on the covers of so many magazines were just a lie. That he deserved to be taken out of circulation, for good. Part of me was reluctant to believe her. Part of me *wanted* to be persuaded. Nobody could be as perfect as Vassilis seemed to be.

Aliki waved her hand to attract the waiter.

"I must get something to eat *right now* – I'm starving! What would you like?"

I was hungry, but the way food was described on the menu made no sense to me. I recognized the names, but not the way they were served. I was used to the kind of place where the proprietor sized you up, decided what you needed, made a note and all you had to do was wait to be served. Job done.

"I don't understand the menu," I told her.

"Oh, me neither. I'm not sure anyone does. It's meant to be international cuisine, recipes from all over the world. Just pick something basic, like chicken; I promise you it's all delicious."

I did as she suggested and sat back while the obviously smitten waiter flapped around Aliki. When he finally got on with his job, I filled her glass and asked an obvious question. The one she still hadn't answered.

"Why meet here? If your husband is as violent as you say he is, won't you having dinner in a place like this only provoke him?"

"I've actually thought of telling him face to face how I feel. Even though he's often told me that he'd kill me if he thought I was going to leave him."

"Are you?"

"Ready to leave him? Yes."

"And as he said he'd kill you, you thought you should be one step ahead."

"If I'm not, I know he'll do it. *I know*. He'll kill me. And he'll find a way to cover it up. He'll manage it like he did with the other two attempts. That's how things are; it's either him or me."

"What attempts?"

"Twice someone's tried to kill me – supposedly."

"Supposedly?"

"They would have succeeded, if they'd really wanted to. They were trying to intimidate me, not kill me. The first time they tampered with my brakes. The second time I'd just come out of a club and this motorcyclist came roaring straight at me."

"That sounds like more than intimidation."

"The brakes weren't completely cut through and I managed to bring the car under control. The motorcyclist swerved to avoid me at the last moment. I'm a very easy target, Mr… sorry, Stratos. Anyone can pick me off. They didn't want to. The motorcyclist then went into a skid on the wet road and was killed by a lorry. The more complicated things are the more Vassilis likes it."

"What made him want to intimidate you?"

"Both attempts occurred after flaming rows. He has these jealous outbursts – one moment he seems normal, the next you don't know what he's going to do. He wanted to terrify me, show me that he could do anything he wanted and then cover it all up – both times the police barely bothered to investigate. And the media didn't even find out about it; usually all we have to do is sneeze to get on the front page."

"Maybe he hushed it up for your sake."

"He would have told me. He never does anything for me without giving me a hard time about it later. He doesn't know how to help someone without some form of payback. That's why I asked to meet you here. Panos, the owner, is one of Vassilis' buddies. Vassilis would never believe I'd dare meet a lover in this of all places. Of course Panos will tell him that I came here with someone, but if he asks – *when* he asks – I can say that you were a producer who wanted to talk about some film. Which is why I asked you to dress for the part. By the way, good clothes suit you. They show off your physique."

There was a playful look in her eyes, which promised nothing and everything. I wondered whether Vassilis was justified in his suspicions. I waited for her to drain yet another glass before she continued.

"Photographs aren't allowed in here, so many celebs come to eat in peace… Panos is really strict about it, he wouldn't even make an exception for Vassilis, and there's no chance of anyone gatecrashing – you need to have connections to get a table here – so my husband's detectives won't know what you look like. And as for anyone I might know here, don't worry, they'll keep a polite distance. That way they can make up any story they like. This restaurant *lives* on speculation and the gossip it arouses. So you see there's no problem… it's as if there's just the two of us here."

She smiled again. Two little dimples appeared on either side of her mouth.

"You seem to have thought of everything," I said.

"My dear husband has trained me well, in his own way. I *have* to think of everything if I want to survive."

"Why don't you go to the police?"

"Do you know how many friends he's got – everywhere? Do you know what close connections he's got with the police and the press? It's not just that they wouldn't lay a finger on him, they'd crucify me on TV and in the newspapers before any court hearing."

"You could divorce him. And get a bodyguard for a year."

"What good would that be? I've heard Vassilis talking on the telephone with everyone from the prime minister to the godfather of the Russian Mafia in Athens. Do you think it would be difficult for him to get rid of a bodyguard? Do you know how many dirty cases he undertakes that he's arranged to keep out of the press? Whatever you think you know about him – his work on behalf of the underdogs – is only what he and his friends allow to be published. When his clients are such big swindlers that the TV channels can't ignore them, he'll send one of his associates as a front man, after he's set everything up intimidating witnesses and jurors. And then, how am I going to pay a bodyguard? Maybe you think I'm loaded, but whatever I have belongs to him."

"Your modelling?"

"Gave it up when I got married. His decision. I'm only on the catwalk for charities – you know, to show how devoted we are to social causes. All those nude and semi-nude photos are from more than three years ago and the magazines just keep reprinting them." She paused. "Have you seen them?"

"I might have caught a glimpse," I said.

"And?"

"They're not bad."

She looked as pleased as a little girl hearing praise for her pigtails. Actually, in one of her photo shoots she did have pigtails, having been dressed as a schoolgirl before she stripped. Another short pause. She finished her glass and poured another one, gazing at me all the time.

"I really loved what was happening then, at the beginning. Everybody – men and women – recognized me from the magazines, they'd turn to get a look at me, wherever it was. I was just eighteen and they chased me like I was the only desirable woman on earth. You can't imagine how many women have given me their numbers hoping I'll phone them. Most of them gorgeous."

"They must have been disappointed when you didn't."

"I don't like to disappoint beautiful people. Why should I deny my body the pleasure?"

"Is that what you think your husband has done to you? Deprived you of pleasure?"

"If you mean that that's the reason why I want him killed, no; I'm not some kind of sex fiend who feels tied by monogamy. Anyway, for someone in your… profession you ask a lot of questions."

"I told you on the phone. First I have to understand *why*. Those are my terms."

"Punctual, discreet meeting place, understanding why… You're full of terms. Don't you ever relax? Maybe you should see my therapist, he's fantastic."

"If you don't like the terms we can leave whenever you like."

"You crazy? I don't miss a meal for anything."

She smiled.

"The truth is that until I met Vassilis I'd only had one other steady relationship, and that didn't last long. I lived to make love. If I was in the mood I could sleep with two or three people a day – ever tried it?"

I made no comment.

"Hope you don't disapprove of what I say and rush off."

"You crazy?" I said. "I don't miss a meal for anything."

She burst out laughing. It felt like collusion, a particularly nice feeling when the colluder's eyes remind you of the sea. Eyes that never laugh, even when the mouth does. Dangerous eyes.

"When I first got to know Vassilis I really fell for him. Well, not him but that public image of his. I bought it completely. I fell for him and cut off my contacts with all the… with the circle of my lovers. I didn't even suspect then that all the donkey work in his office – the poor, underprivileged stuff – is done by his staff, leaving his time free for the big boys. Most of the big corporations he's beaten in court are now his best customers."

"What does your husband know about your previous relationships?"

I was careful not to mention him by name. I never mention the name of my targets before a hit. I don't want to feel any connection.

"Not much. He couldn't take it."

"How do you know that?"

"Recently he came home early and caught me watching a video an old lover and I had made with one of my fans."

"You mean…?"

"In bed, yes. We'd tied up the girl and were… just messing about really, having fun. No violence, though. I can't stand it. Vassilis went ballistic; he didn't even know that I'd had a relationship with… this big-shot banker, anyway, no need to mention names. Neither did he know anything about the women in my life. I told him that what he saw was a one-off. He didn't hit me much, compared with other times, he just kicked my legs and stomach, but afterwards he locked me in the bedroom for two days, without food. When I protested he said: 'You don't need it. From what I saw you've already eaten well enough.' The first evening I had my ear glued to the door, trying to find out what he was doing. He'd put on the video and was watching it over and over again. He's crazy, and he *wants* me to know it. When he finally opened the door he was all affection. He'd bought me flowers, he promised to take me on a holiday so that we could get away and relax, he'd cooked my favourite dish, he wanted us to make love… no mention at all of the previous two days. Me neither; dangerous waters. I avoided him, saying I had a headache, and went to bed. I was so worn out by the stress and crying of those two days that I went straight to sleep. Next day I awoke at noon, to find that he'd left a novel by my bed, with a bookmark. I opened it and he'd underlined something in red. It said: 'You will be mine forever. Whatever it takes.'"

Wonderful people, wonderful world. My contribution is to select some of them for liquidation. I'm a kind of social worker, except I get properly paid. I remembered a line from *The Two Jakes*, one of my favourite films: "Hell, everybody makes mistakes. But if you marry one, they expect you to pay for it for the rest of your life."

"Any other reasons why you want to leave him?" I asked.

"Are any more needed?"

"Just because there aren't doesn't mean they don't exist."

Her mobile rang. Irritably, she snapped open her bag, took out the phone, checked the screen, and switched it off.

"I never answer when I see a hidden caller ID."

"Fans?"

"I don't know. And I don't want to. Look, since you're asking me about other reasons... if you're thinking that I'm doing this for money, forget it. Some of my exes, among the richest men in the country, have proposed to me. Some of them persisted in proposing even *after* I married Vassilis. I don't have to kill anybody to get money, Stratos. You've seen my photos... I want my life back, that's all. I just want my life back."

It sounded like a good enough reason to me.

"Since you mentioned money..." I said.

"Yes?"

"I'm not cheap."

"I didn't expect you to be."

"And with this particular target... I might have to disappear for a while."

"I understand."

"Which means…"

I grabbed a napkin, took a pen from my jacket pocket and wrote two numbers, one the down payment, the other the total. I never *say* how much I want; I write it down for the client to read and agree to. That becomes my contract.

"It's a lot, but I'll find it," she said.

"How?"

"You need to know that, too?"

"You said your husband controls your money. And even if I manage to make it seem like an accident, the cops will investigate all possibilities."

"I can imagine, but…"

"The wife is always the prime suspect. They'll visit the banks. They'll ask to check your accounts, both joint and personal. If they see that you've withdrawn a large sum they'll be on to you. That could lead them to me. Which I can't allow to happen."

"You mean that…"

She pointed to herself, asking if I meant that I'd rub her out, if necessary. Fear could be a useful lever. I nodded.

I suspected that she'd get the cash from one of her loaded ex-lovers who was itching to be back with her. If she confirmed that was her intention, I'd wash my hands of her.

"The money won't come from my account," she said. "My friend Lena will lend it to me. You know, the one who spoke with your… lady friend and put us in touch."

I nodded. Second time she hesitated when referring to Teri. At least she got the sex right.

"Lena's the only one who knows everything about me – we've been best friends ever since we met at university – she finished, I dropped out. She got married last year to a tycoon, who's really mad about her, lets her spend as much as she likes. Whatever I ask her for she'll give me. Is that OK?"

Before I answered her question I had one more of my own.

"Why are you so sure you can trust me? You just said that whatever you've got belongs to your husband. What's to stop me telling him the whole story in return for a stack of dough?"

Bitter smile. A gulp of wine. "Because you were recommended by Lena, who loves me. Because talking to you makes me feel confident. And, mainly, because I don't have any alternative. I trust you because I have to."

That seemed convincing enough. I nodded.

"OK, check with your friend about the money and we'll arrange the deposit. In the meantime, I need to know your husband's daily routine. Have you written it down?"

She took out a piece of paper from her bag and slipped it to me just as our starters arrived. The waiter was looking at her, while trying to pretend that he noticed my existence.

I don't generally get on with clients. One reason is that most of them are not the types you have a good time with. Usually I'm impatient for the meeting to end. I don't believe in mixing business with pleasure. Which is why I was surprised when the rest of the evening passed quicker than any other I could remember for a while. We ate, drank, told stories – her mostly, I just mentioned a couple of things that happened to Teri and me when we were at school. We were like two strangers who meet in the middle of nowhere and discover that they think the same way and have the same sense of humour.

As her husband was waiting for her at home – not for much longer, if I did my job – Aliki asked for the bill.

"How will I get in touch with you?" she said.

"When necessary, I'll phone you. Like yesterday," I said.

"I'd feel better if there was some way of contacting you."

"In an emergency, call Teri."

"I mean direct."

"Impossible."

"Another condition?"

She gave me a disapproving smile. She had a whole armoury of smiles at her disposal. She offered me her hand, to say goodbye. It smelt of jasmine.

"I'll expect your call," she said.

I nodded.

I watched as she walked away. Allowing her time to leave, I went to the bathroom, splashed some water on my face and stared at it in the mirror. I remembered a line from another film, *Double Indemnity*. "I killed him for money and for a woman. I didn't get the money. And I didn't get the woman."

I had no intention of making the same mistake. I'd concentrate on the money. I'd take it and forget the woman.

Glancing back as I left, I saw the name of the restaurant. "La Luna". "The Moon". Glowing in neon. Anyone who wants to see the real moon grabs a snack and stretches out on the nearest patch of grass. Those who are not so keen on reality go and eat incomprehensible food at five-star restaurants on Sacred Way Street.

I looked around. An unmarked police car was parked at the junction of Sacred Way and Constantinople. I'd seen it before. The driver got out and came towards me. Tall – almost as tall as myself, but much thinner. Thinning blond hair, slightly round-shouldered, he was wearing a white raincoat that was much too long for him.

"Mr Gazis?"

"That's me."

"Costas Dragas. Athens Police. We'd like you to accompany us."

"Who's 'we'?"

"Officers. Everywhere. You're surrounded."

"Looks like I have no choice, then. Where are we going?"

"Souvlaki?"

"Just ate."

"When did that ever stop you?"

"I'd prefer pizza."

"Since I'm hungrier shouldn't I make the choice?"

"OK. What's with your raincoat?"

"What do you mean?"

"Shabby, grubby, made for someone twice your size."

He looked down as if seeing it for the first time.

"I'll take it off," he said.

Costas Dragas, or "Drag" as everybody knew him at school. After only a short while in the force he had made such an impression that he could choose whatever division he wanted to work in. They really wanted him in Narcotics but he chose Homicide and was talked of as the best they'd ever had. And he'd stayed my best mate; the best cop and the best caretaker. Ironic.

5

You never forget the day you met your best friend.

The three thugs who surrounded the boy and his sister were shaven-headed. They were all twice the size of the boy, who was tall but slight. The street was empty. Rarely does the temperature in Athens drop below freezing, but that winter was one of the coldest recorded. I had the silent streets pretty much to myself. A joy, to be one of the city's shadows.

"So, this your little sister?" one of them said to the boy, reaching out his hand to stroke her cheek. "Real cute."

The frightened girl flinched and hid behind her brother.

"Shy, too," said the one who seemed to be the leader. The other two stood around sniggering.

"I like them shy. They scream more. Do you like to scream, cutie?"

"Look at those juicy little lips, how they're trembling!"

"Get lost!" said the boy, who appeared to be about my age, early teens. The thugs fell about laughing.

"The big man's giving us orders!" the leader spluttered, slurring his words.

"Get lost!" one of the others mimicked in a high voice.

They guffawed.

"I'm not going to tell you again," said the boy.

"Because I'm kind-hearted I'll give you a choice," the leader responded.

They couldn't see me standing at the corner of the street. Dressed all in black, I had melted into the night. The only dim light in the street was over the group. I put my hand into my pocket and gripped my army knife.

"You can join in," the leader said to the boy. "We'll go off in our lorry over there, choose a nice place and, after we three are done fucking Cutie's brains out, we'll let you give it to her. You've dreamt about it, right? Me, in your place, with a sister like that, I'd think of nothing else. And afterwards, if you behave, we'll let you go. We'll even take you back home, so that we know where we can find you."

"Yeah, yeah," said one of the others. "Maybe Cutie will tell her mum what a good time she had and mum will want some too."

The boy just stared at them.

"OK," said the leader, signalling their attack.

They weren't quick enough. The boy leapt into action, punching one of them in the neck and toppling the other with a kick behind the knee. The first one was out cold and the second stayed where he was after a kick in the face. But the leader didn't just stand there. He grabbed hold of the girl and put a gun to her head.

"Well done, warrior boy! Who do you want to die first – you or her?"

The boy, helpless, stared at him and the sobbing girl in his arms.

"Please... please, we haven't done anything to you," she said in a voice that trembled almost as much as she did.

"YOU OR HER?"

"Me," said the boy.

"Good choice."

He turned the gun on the boy but let out a scream as I knifed him in the back. He tried to turn to look at me but I thrust the knife in deeper. He collapsed at my feet, the gun falling from his hands. I'd pierced his lungs. Blood gushed out of his mouth and nose. He struggled to breathe but all he could do was make a gurgling sound, the sound of someone drowning in his own blood.

I turned to look at the boy and his sister. The girl was sobbing, her brother was trying to calm her. He stared at me, still on the alert.

"It seemed like you needed some help," I said.

"Thanks."

He held out his hand. I held out mine.

"Costas," he said.

"Stratos. Nice to meet you."

6

Drag is the second person I would trust with my eyes closed.
Those three punks, twenty years ago, brought us together
and we became inseparable. We soon discovered that we
lived close to each other and I changed schools to be with
him. Teri then raised our little gang's number by one. The
alphabetical system for sorting pupils into classes helped
us to spend every day together: Dragas, Gazis and Berikis,
the second, third and fourth letters in the Greek alphabet.
Lefteris Berikis – that was Teri, when she still wore a goatee.

Drag has no problem with my profession. So long as
I take care of people who deserve it, as he puts it, he has
no reason to intervene. Though he often intervenes to
protect me.

Like my last job with Yevgeni, a fine Russian fellow who,
with his gang of equally admirable associates, tried to break
into the protection racket in the city centre. One of the
bar owners refused to give way to their threats. Yevgeni
and his mates turned up late at his bar and explained
succinctly to the customers that they should leave, and
held the owner, the barman and a waitress captive. Later,
one of the men brought in the owner's wife and five-year-
old girl, bound with rope. They took turns raping them
for three hours in front of him and then executed them,

shooting the daughter in the head and clubbing the wife to death. Then they left the owner and his staff tied up and blew the place up. The other bar owners got together, approached and hired me, and now Yevgeni can't rape and murder five-year-old girls any more. The evening I went to visit him, however, I nearly joined Yevgeni in his journey to the other world. Luckily, Drag, armed with a high-precision Harrington & Richardson rifle, was watching events from a building opposite the warehouse where I had arranged to meet Yevgeni. Drag put two bullets in the neck of one of Yevgeni's men who had crept up on me unawares. Before leaving, I stood over Yevgeni's dead body and shot his head to a pulp. Sometimes you can be excused for going over the top.

Drag and I had arrived in Sacred Way Street much earlier than his colleagues. One of Drag's snitches had tipped him off that a killer was posing as a refugee among the immigrants in the building that was to be evacuated. A killer who had escaped from a Syrian prison and had joined the jihadists. The Greek government was already receiving a lot of heat after the terrorist attack in Paris, where one of the jihadists was revealed to have entered Europe through Greece, as a refugee. Drag didn't give a rat's arse about any Greek government, but he didn't like killers lurking around his city. So he went, and I joined him. We work together, backing each other in our jobs when we get the chance. Unfortunately, I can't help Drag as much as I'd like – when the time comes for action, he is usually accompanied by hordes of cops. It's not a great idea for me to mingle with them, especially since some of them have their sights fixed on being number one and are waiting for Drag to make the slightest slip-up, to bring him down. Luckily, my friend's adventurous nature leads him to undertake some missions on his own. He's earned that right with his successes.

Drag kicked open the door of the apartment where the Syrian would be hiding, only to hear a baby's cry. That could have been a ploy from the Syrian to get us to let down our guard. Drag went in, with me covering his back, but we found no Syrian killer. A gaunt, dark-skinned woman was lying at the far end of the room, breastfeeding a baby. Another baby, the twin of the first, was lying dead beside her. These little rooms were usually packed with refugees, but the babies and their mother were so sick that the other immigrants had allowed them their own space, to avoid infection and to let them die in peace.

Drag took the mother and the baby to the hospital, gave his snitch a piece of his mind and returned to Sacred Way Street to wait for me to finish my meeting at the restaurant. As usual, he had a crime novel to read. He didn't have much of a social life.

I'm not sure why I asked for his help. How dangerous could a meeting with Aliki Stylianou be? I asked myself that question many times during the following, totally crazy days.

7

We had just got into Drag's black Nissan when my mobile phone rang. The screen showed that Teri was calling. I put the phone to Drag's ear.

"Who is it?" he asked suspiciously.

"Really pretty girl. Say something nice," I whispered.

"Hello," he growled.

When he realized it was Teri his face flushed with anger. They'd quarrelled over all kinds of little things ever since their schooldays. They quarrelled and made up so often that usually they didn't know what state they were in and waited for the other's reaction to determine how they should behave. Their latest row had happened two weeks earlier, during one of our regular poker games at Teri's place. Drag had a terrible run and kept on losing all night until, just as we were reaching the end of the game, he found himself with four eights. He didn't care about money, but he hated to lose. Teri had won most of his chips, but he staked about a third of what he had left to prevent her from suspecting he had a monster hand. I folded straight away. Teri squinted at Drag through half-closed eyes – we were all smashed – and smiled.

"See you and raise you whatever you've got left," she said.

The best hand that had appeared all evening was a low full house. Drag thought with his four-of-a-kind he was king. He pushed the rest of his chips to the centre of the table, turned over his cards with a howl of victory and kicked away his chair to celebrate.

"Mmm… very good. But not good enough," Teri said, revealing four nines.

Drag just stood there, gobsmacked. Slowly, he managed to locate his chair and lower himself into it, without once taking his eyes off the cards.

If the scene had ended there everything would have been alright, but it didn't. Many things have changed about Teri but not the competitive characteristic she has had in common with Drag since childhood. She let out a howl of her own, then showed off by turning a double somersault, pulled up her blouse, whipped off her bra and revealed her newly acquired knockers. She wiggled them in front of Drag, who, despite the many things he has seen, remains deeply conservative. In a state of shock, he got up and left without saying another word. He hadn't spoken to Teri for two weeks. In a way, I understood him. However much you love a person, as we did Teri, however much you know, as we did, growing up with her, that all her characteristics are female and that her birth as a boy was one of nature's mistakes, there is a limit to what you can accept. Not that it is easy to explain that to her. Even after Drag had stormed out that night, all Teri could say, still showing off her breasts, was, "What's got into him? Don't tell me they're not convincing or I'll lie down and die."

*

I was already grinning in expectation of an outburst from Drag when his expression changed. Something was going on. He handed me the phone and accelerated away. By the time Teri had explained, we had already reached the top of Achilles Street, turned right and were heading full speed towards Karaiskaki Square.

8

The square was so quiet there was no need for him to slow down. Outside a high-class clothes shop with a green neon sign I caught sight of two homeless people, a man and a woman, spreading their blankets next to each other. All their possessions were next to them in two black rubbish bags. You rarely see two homeless people together, they're usually solitary and like to monopolize their little corners and benches. Once I had found my mum in that state. Alone. All her possessions stuffed into one of my old schoolbags.

We soon found ourselves at the crossroads between Favierou and Mayer. The police station was less than three minutes away but Drag was the only policeman around and he was officially off-duty.

Teri had given Drag accurate directions. Aliki's 4x4, a brand-new silver BMW X5, was stationed diagonally in the middle of the crossroads. It was peppered with bullet holes. The only living thing around was a large stray dog, looking for scraps. A shower of bullets has a tendency to empty places. Especially in Athens, the Balkan centre of the Kalashnikov trade. The guns were favoured by foreigners working for Greek gangsters, but anyone can become a victim in this city.

It wasn't really my business to be there with Drag. I wasn't under any obligation, I hadn't decided whether or not to take the contract and I hadn't received any money. If a contract is cancelled, I do what every other worker does – go and look for another job. The employer's problems are really no business of mine. I would help Drag, if he needed me. And I'd get Aliki Stylianou out of my mind.

Drag parked about fifty feet from the BMW and whipped out a Glock 26. He didn't like heavy weapons, unlike me who can't take a step without my favourite Sig Sauer P226.40 S&W when I'm on the job. When you're not an expert marksman and your hands are too big for most firearms, you need the best gun to ensure the job will get done, even if you don't hit the bullseye. Drag, on the contrary, never misses. Except once. When Teri was still working the streets, Ayis, a young pimp, and two of his bouncer friends, had tried to hustle her into giving him a cut of her takings. Some girls who had refused ended up in hospital. As Teri was one against three, she managed to restrain herself and asked us to intervene. Drag had suggested scaring off Ayis, but the bullet he claimed was meant to go wide ended up in Ayis' head. Drag still says he missed. I pretend to believe him.

I stayed behind Drag to cover him, but I was ready to disappear if a cop who was actually on duty suddenly showed up. I've never been arrested but there was no reason to get involved in explanations of who I was and what I was doing there.

Drag opened the 4x4's door on the driver's side. I saw him pick up a woman's body, lay it gently on the pavement and bend over it.

Eyes like the sea.

He's often told me that he'd kill me if he thought I was going to leave him. And he'll find a way to cover it up.

The scent of jasmine.

Dimples.

A little black bag with huge gold lettering.

I walked towards Drag. He was feeling her neck for a sign of a pulse, but we both knew it was useless. I wanted to look away, but I couldn't.

She was very beautiful, even in death. Her face was pale, as though she was asleep. There was a small black hole at the base of her neck. Her killers weren't satisfied with the Kalashnikov; they wanted to make sure with another shot at closer range.

A police siren made me straighten up. Drag and I exchanged confused looks.

Because the body at our feet wasn't Aliki Stylianou.

9

Every man meets three important women in his life, and I learnt from a film how to know if you'd just met one of them.

It was *A Bronx Tale*, directed by Robert De Niro. You have a date with a girl. You park your car, get out, lock it and go off to fetch her. When you bring her back to the car you open her door and let her in. Then you walk around and look through the rear window. If she doesn't lean over to unlock your door you should dump her fast, however much you fancy her. If she *does* open it, she could be the woman of your life.

It works. I know, because I tried it when I was seventeen.

Maria Armyrou came to our school when we were in sixth form. Morning assembly was over and there was a lot of noise as we waited for our first lesson. It was philosophy, with a sweet old man who often dozed off and only really got our attention when he came up close to our desks stinking of garlic. When Maria appeared – she'd transferred from her school in Rhodes, where her father was a tax collector – the noise faded to a hush. A hush of desire from the boys. A hush of jealousy from the girls. Over the next two years Maria was lusted after by every boy in the area, including Drag and Teri, who, though she has a clear preference for men, never says no to a beautiful woman.

Maria Armyrou was chestnut blond, with deep green eyes, sensual lips and a toned body that was the result of exercise she took for its own sake, as competitiveness bored her. She could translate Ancient Greek, solve unbelievably difficult geometry problems, and hold her own in rough football games with boys twice her size, scoring from every position with her amazing left foot. She was the best student when she could be bothered, but when she wasn't she played truant.

Maria Armyrou leant over and unlocked the driver's door for me. Without having seen the film. She's the third person, after Teri and Drag, who I would trust my life with. She's also the only important woman in my life, as I'm still waiting for the other two.

Leaving Stylianou's bullet-riddled car I went straight to Maria's. We're neighbours. The place I live in, a flat in Psychiko, belongs to her. Her and her husband.

"Can you start at the beginning, I'm confused," Maria said.

"OK."

It was three o'clock in the morning. Quite normal for a night bird like Maria. She doesn't sleep till she sees the sun rise.

"Stylianou found you through Teri and you met at La Luna. Drag was waiting for you outside."

It was good that she could say his name. For a long time Drag and Maria couldn't bear to mention each other. The reason why Maria and I had separated was much simpler. Though we'd fallen in love when we were young, we'd discovered two things. The first was that we loved each other a lot and weren't going to stop feeling that way; the second was that we couldn't bear to live together as a couple.

A Bronx Tale was right. It just didn't specify that the woman of your life may not be the one you spend your life with.

It took Drag a long time before he dared make his move. First he cleared it with me; stammering and stuttering, as if he needed my permission. Then he told Maria how he felt – in a letter, because he couldn't bring himself to do it face to face. They stayed together for five years and separated for reasons I'm still not sure about. Drag withdrew into himself more than ever. Then Maria met Sotiris, a very intelligent, funny guy. His wheelchair didn't deter her at all. They got married after a few months and I know that they are still very much in love.

"So was La Luna crowded?"

"Not an empty table."

"So much for the financial crisis. And you and Stylianou left separately so that her husband's spies wouldn't see you together," continued Maria.

"It was her suggestion."

"And the next thing is Teri phones Drag to say that Stylianou had called, terrified, pleading for help and telling Teri where she was."

"Yes."

"Drag was off duty. You hadn't agreed to do the job but, even if you had, you're not Stylianou's bodyguard. So, why did you go?"

Like Drag and Teri, Maria has no objection to my work. She thinks it's useful – "noble" she called it once – the way I operate. She may be influenced by the fact that, twenty years ago, one of her uncles raped her teenage sister, screwing her up so much she's been in and out of institutions ever since, and has to live on her parents' pension – whatever's left of it. The uncle was sent to prison for a few years and Maria was just waiting for him to come out so that she could kill him with her own hands. His heart attack, the day before he was due to be released, robbed her of justice.

Why did we go? Maria always asks the right questions. For me the answer was relatively simple: I got too close to Aliki Stylianou that evening to ignore her call for help. A woman who only has someone like me to turn to, who is so desperate she phones Teri, a transsexual prostitute she's never met, is a woman so alone even I could bend my professional rules. Being a very beautiful woman also helped. Yet, despite all that, I'm not sure I would have gone if I hadn't been with Drag. And what I couldn't tell Maria without hurting her was that, ever since they separated, Drag is never really off duty. He's become indifferent to *life*, outside work. That's why he raced to the junction of Favierou and Mayer when he heard Teri on the phone.

"So? If it was none of your business, why did you go?" Maria repeated, seeing my hesitation.

"Professional perversion," I replied, putting on a – hopefully persuasive – grin.

10

Maria quickly made me an omelette and left the kitchen to help Sotiris with his bath. They stay up late together, having epic chess and draughts battles, listening to music, watching films, trying to beat each other's scores on their iPads. Sotiris' parents have properties that they rent out in and around Athens, and are sufficiently well-off to ensure he'd never have to work if he was a little careful with his money. Maria works occasionally as a graphic designer and consultant for an English publisher. They love her work, but she only takes jobs when she feels like it or needs some extra cash. Sotiris trained as a teacher but he doesn't teach. Not because he's an invalid. He just prefers spending all day with Maria. I don't blame him.

Sotiris knows that I'm one of Maria's old friends, that I make enough to get by, and that I keep myself to myself, which is why I don't invite people home. We get along alright. Just.

As I was eating, I kept gazing at my mobile phone. Still no news from Drag. I went to the sink to wash the plates. From Maria's kitchen window you look straight into the flat opposite where, every night, in the small hours, a fat middle-aged man and a haggard dark-haired woman make love with the curtains open and lights blazing. Perhaps they don't think anyone's watching at that time of night, or would be interested. The ugliness of their entwined bodies has a richness you don't get in romantic films, with their body-perfect actors.

I left them to it and opened the back door, which leads by a long flight of steps into the storage room. I went down the first eight, stopped at the mezzanine between the ground and first floor, bent down and felt around the bottom of the wall. The button I was searching for was small and white, and like the door of my flat, practically invisible. I pressed the button and the electronic device I had installed in place of a door handle appeared. I put my hand in the proper position on the device, waited five seconds for it to recognize me, and the door opened. It's the only way of getting in. Maria has allowed me to arrange my place to cater for the demands of my profession. Security. A very expensive story. I would like to have more windows than just the one in my flat, to be able to throw them all open and let the air sweep through, to strip naked and feel it on my body, like I did as a kid, my mum chasing me with my clothes. But it would make the flat vulnerable. The area outside my only window is full of sensors that warn me of any irregular movement. For years I have been making sure that nobody knows where I live, with the exception of my friends. Even the address I declare in all the official papers under my new name is different. I don't want to put Maria in danger. If anything happens I have to be ready.

I shut the door behind me and experienced the sense of relief I always feel, seeing the room clean and tidy. Every room I've occupied since I was a boy has been neat and uncluttered. Order helps me think.

My phone was still mute. There were two choices. The first was to wait for news from Drag. By morning the dead girl would have been identified and the cops would be looking for Aliki, the owner of the BMW. The second choice was to phone Aliki herself. To ask her what happened, if she was OK and still wanted to go ahead with our arrangement. It would show her I was interested.

Been to the hospital twice with fractures. He only hits me on the body, so that he can palm off my injuries as some kind of accident.

Two choices, one obvious answer.

If someone needs you they will find you.

Don't take useless steps.

And never, *never*, get close to a client.

I looked at the mobile phone.

I waited.

11

I was more tired than I thought. In my dream, Maria came to help me take a bath and was amazed to discover that my legs had healed. She called me Sotiris and I thought that I ought to put her right but I didn't because it didn't bother me; she could call me any name she wanted as long as she stayed with me. Just as we were getting together in the bath to celebrate, her face changed into that of Aliki. It was terribly scarred and out of her swollen mouth came the mutilated word "help". Then she gave me a bitter smile that hurt worse than the most heart-breaking tears. As the smile became wider and wider, the scars on her face seemed to multiply. Luckily, at that point, my mobile rang and woke me. Luckily, because such dreams have tortured me ever since I realized that I've never stopped being in love with Maria and made a terrible mistake in letting her go.

It was Teri on the phone, her annoyance crackling over the line.

"I want a word with you."

"That's six already."

"Am I your secretary now?"

"What's the matter?"

"Stylianou phoned back. I was with *him*."

He was Nikos Zois, the guy Teri was recently crazy about. I hadn't met him yet, but she couldn't stop gushing about what a great guy he was, as well as being a hunk.

"I'm sorry."

"*You* are sorry? He had just an hour between meetings and came to see me, and…"

"Tell you anything important?"

"Nikos?"

"Stylianou."

"Ah… yes. She said she was alright, she's hiding somewhere, and that she wanted to talk to you. She sounded shit scared."

12

"Elsa Dalla, thirty-two years old," Drag said.

It was midnight on a melancholy, pitch-black night, and I had suggested we drop by the Serbetia café in the Psyrri district, to talk while eating chocolate-orange pie with vanilla ice cream. He insisted that we should go to our usual haunt, Papi's, a coffee bar close to my place, open 24/7. Drag had the results of the post-mortem: the ballistics report showed that the bullets were from an AK-47, as expected, and there were no witnesses, as expected. What we didn't expect was that the La Luna waiter would have such a good memory. The description he gave of my face to the guy who did mugshot sketches was perfect, Drag told me. I was one of the last people to see Aliki before Dalla's body was found in her car. So the police needed a statement from me, and if they couldn't find me they'd release the sketch to the media, asking for anyone who knew me to come forward. I wasn't a murder suspect. Aliki wasn't the victim and we had left separately, as the doorman at La Luna testified. However, Drag advised me to lie low while they were combing Athens for evidence – and forget eating chocolate pastries around Psyrri. You never know who might claim to have seen me.

The chairs in Papi's seem to be from the seventies – retro style, scratched wood, torn covering. The decor is brown and white – it may have started white, but decades of smokers have darkened it. Papi, the owner, fits right in – his Greek father got to know his African mother while visiting Congo in the 1940s to find a mining job and they stayed together till she died. Papi, who was born on the day the Second World War ended, looks like a pygmy, barely five feet tall. Under his snow-white hair he has a funny face with little eyebrows, pop eyes and bulging cheeks, which becomes even funnier when he frowns, realizing that he's mixed up the orders again. He is very discreet, though, and Drag and I feel at ease there. We don't hide the fact that we are friends, but we do understand that our public appearances together don't exactly improve either Drag's professional image, or mine.

Apart from his discretion, Papi's major attraction is a jukebox, an imposing grey Seeburg M100B Select-O-Matic circa 1950, the first model to play 45s and the first to be so well designed that it allowed discs to be played vertically, extending the choice of songs from twenty to 100. Papi tells most people that it cost a fortune to get it sent from America, but to us he confided that he found it up for auction on eBay and discovered that the guy who owned it was an old friend who owed him a big favour from their time in the Congo. That's how favours are, like cats; however far they stray they find their way back home. Drag and I happened to be there when it was delivered. Papi stroked it tenderly, then went to turn it on, only to discover that it only took American five-cent coins, a fact his Congolese friend had forgotten to mention. Papi spent weeks searching for nickels, but he got there in the end. We were the guests of honour at the machine's inauguration. We were also the *only* guests. Papi is even more of a loner than we are. His first choice, once the jukebox had swallowed his five cents, was Sinatra's *Moonlight Serenade*. As he listened, with rapturously closed eyes, I could have sworn that he grew several inches taller. After the song finished, he unlocked the machine's cashbox. Anyone who wants to use the jukebox has to collect their nickels from Papi.

Drag and I disagreed violently over what was the most moving performance ever of a blues song. Drag nearly wore down the needle playing Ella Fitzgerald's *Every Time We Say Goodbye*, while I couldn't stop playing *Cry Me a River* by Dinah Washington. I think we overdid it one day, because Papi presented each of us with our preferred disc "as a present". While Drag and I were trying to imagine what our life in Papi's would be like without Ella or Dinah, Papi went to the jukebox and put on *I'm a Fool to Want You*, sung by Billie Holiday – who only lived forty-four tortured years but managed to change the way in which people listened to jazz. On Papi's disc her voice is worn by the rape and beatings she received from the men in her life, by booze and drugs. You almost can't recognize it. And from the first phrase, what remains of her voice becomes greater than it had ever been. It was the most moving performance Drag and I ever heard. We put down our own discs on the table, stopped bickering and listened to Lady Day, dead for fifty years, filling that shabby old coffee bar in Athens.

"Elsa Dalla? Sounds like a fake name to me," I told Drag.

"Like you have a good ear."

"Thanks."

"Maybe you should have been a musician."

"A maestro."

"Actually, do you know why the Venetians named a wind the 'maestral'?"

"I don't think about winds that often."

"Because it is the master-wind. *Maestro*. Not to be confused with the French mistral wind, which is very different," he said.

"Is that relevant to our case?"

"Not at all."

"OK, then."

Drag loves to share with his friends any information he picks up, anytime it pops into his head.

"Her real name was Evanthia Markantonopoulou."

"I'm not surprised she changed it."

"'Elsa Dalla' was dreamt up by the director of her TV series when she was brought to him to get her a part."

"Brought to him?"

"She was sleeping with the producer."

"Well done, Evanthia. What's his name?"

"Tassos Regoudis. Haven't seen him yet. The Chief said he's too big a name to be hauled in for questioning."

"Never heard of him."

"I spoke to one of his lawyers. He announced that Dr Regoudis would see me at twelve o'clock tomorrow, at his house."

"Doctor?"

"He has a doctorate in biology from some Romanian university. He's had the certificate blown up and framed in his office and insists on people calling him doctor."

"And you got to know all that from...?"

"The director. The one who thought of the name 'Elsa Dalla'. A certain… Peppas. Hermes Peppas. Apparently he was about to resign because of the constant pressure Regoudis was putting on the writers to make Elsa's part bigger."

"At least he won't have to worry about that any more."

"He's keen to cooperate, in case I make him a suspect."

"Do you suspect him?"

"Probably not. He's an *artist*."

"Artists can be killers. But what about Stylianou? What's she got to do with…?"

"Nikolidaga."

"What?"

"Aliki Nikolidaga. Her real name. Seems like nobody in showbiz sticks to their real name."

"Right. While you, *Drag…*"

He shot me a look. I went back to the murder before he got angry; when you stir Drag up it's like a tidal wave that comes and goes.

"So? What did Stylianou, whose real name is Nikolidaga, have to do with Dalla, whose real name is Markantonopoulou?"

"Besides the fact they look very alike I don't know yet. I've had a word with Peppas and with five of the actors. They all told me that Dalla and Stylianou were polite to each other, nothing more. They never went around together, nor did they bitch about each other. There was no reason for jealousy because Aliki had a very small part in the series. But I can't get hold of her or her husband. Their mobiles are switched off, nobody answers at their house, and if I actually asked them to come to the station and make a statement, I'd be transferred to the Greek–Turkish border in no time. If they warned me to treat Regoudis gently, think what would happen with Stathopoulos... All I've found out is that Aliki doesn't have any close relations. She's an only child, whose parents were killed in a road accident some years ago, close to their home in Patras. So the only thing I've got, so far, is an ambitious but little-known actress, playing a bit part in a TV series, professionally bumped off in a car belonging to a model who's just started her acting career. Any ideas, Mr Caretaker?"

"None whatsoever."

Not far from us, Papi was sitting reading a newspaper. On the jukebox, Louis Armstrong was singing that life was a cabaret. Not for Elsa Dalla it wasn't.

13

There's always a fine line in the relationships between best friends, and it grows even thinner when your professions aren't exactly compatible. For example, when we work together as a team, Drag and I are more or less invincible. But if I had told him that I knew where Aliki Stylianou was hiding and that I was going to meet her later, then Drag would have felt obliged to get to her before I did. And I never betray a client, unless they betray me first.

Aliki Stylianou hadn't betrayed me.

I'd phoned her immediately after speaking to Teri. She hadn't picked up the phone, but called me back when I was with Drag at Papi's. I stood up casually, to avoid alerting him, and moved to the back of the bar, where he couldn't hear me.

"Stratos," I said.

I heard a sigh of relief from the other end.

"Thank God it's you. Can you come?"

"Where?"

"I'm scared, really scared and I can't..."

She gave a sob, then pulled herself together.

"I don't know what to do, where to go... They killed that girl... thought it was me... he killed her..."

Drag was staring at me. I put on a smile.

"Your husband?"

"Yes. Now I have proof."

"Then you can go to the police. We're not talking about his threats any more. With the murder, they'll listen to you."

"No, no, not the police, it'll never get to court, he'll destroy me, he'll turn everything upside down and get them all behind him, no…"

What she said next was unintelligible. She was hysterical. I waited. At first her words were muffled by sobs but gradually sense began to emerge.

"I… I phoned him… from a shop… said I was alright but… scared because of what had happened, and… and that I was going to… to hide. Then I… took a taxi… got as far from there as I could… I… I w… wanted him to think that I didn't know – that he was behind it… that I was frightened of an unknown killer."

"What happened after you left the restaurant? Why was that girl in your car?"

"I'll explain… when you come. You'll come, right? I need… protection… Please, *please*…"

I told her I'd be there in an hour. Had to show no sign of urgency, to put Drag off the scent. When I returned to the table and he asked who was on the phone, I told him it was Maria. That ended that conversation.

I drive a blue Peugeot 206, which, for security reasons, officially belongs to a senile older cousin. One of my accounts in Zurich is also under the same name; it's the one where I get my clients to deposit their payments, if they have accounts abroad. For those restricted by the capital controls, I am willing to take cash. I got into the car, turned on the light, and looked through the newspaper to see which pharmacies were open that night. In my job that's useful information if I get injured away from home. My flat is equipped like a small hospital to deal with any emergency.

Driving towards my meeting with Aliki, I searched the radio for some good jazz. Nothing. I made do with pop songs from the eighties and nineties, the ones my generation grew up with. At least they weren't in short supply.

A few minutes later I noticed a car tailing me, at a distance. It wasn't difficult to recognize Drag's black Nissan.

14

I jammed the car into the first space I found in the narrow road. Drag did the same, 100 yards behind. The street lights were dim – very dim for such a dark night. The municipality was short of cash, or someone was embezzling it. Or both. I took my mobile phone out of my pocket and called Drag. He answered on the third ring.

"Hey."

"How stupid can you be?"

"Very."

"At least you admit it. Get your arse over here."

"You get yours here – right now," he said.

His tone convinced me that something was up. Maybe it was nothing – Drag could be temperamental, or maybe he'd suddenly had an idea he wanted to talk about – but it never hurts to be prepared. The Sig Sauer was on the seat next to me – even in my shoulder holster it was heavy, so I decided to leave it where it was. I had a leg holster with a Smith & Wesson 642. I took out the gun and stuffed it in my jacket pocket. Then I slowly walked towards Drag's car. If everything was OK he would get out, light a cigarette, and wait for me. A simple code between friends who have been through a lot together. Drag didn't get out. I kept my hand in my pocket and approached the passenger door.

Drag was looking annoyed. Annoyed, not frightened, in spite of the gun pressed to the bottom of his skull. The gun was held by one of two people sitting in the back seat, a big solid man with cropped hair, prominent cheekbones and cold green eyes. He looked a bit like me. I remembered an exchange in *White Heat*, where Roy Parker asks Cody Jarrett whether he would kill him in cold blood. "Oh, no," says Jarrett. "I'll let you warm up a little."

One glance at the guy with the gun was enough to know he didn't share Cody Jarrett's sense of humour.

The gunman's boss was sitting next to him with a slight smile on his face. He had dark features and a full head of hair, impeccably styled and just touched with grey. I wouldn't have called him handsome, but he'd stand out in a crowd. It's a quality I lack and am a little jealous of. This guy was known all over Greece. Despite that, he introduced himself.

"I'm Vassilis Stathopoulos," he said. "Let's talk."

15

"Mr Gazis, there are many things you don't know."

"About life?"

Our happy little company had been transferred to Stathopoulos' mansion in Voula, following his polite proposal. When someone's holding a gun to your head, you have a tendency to accept their proposal, polite or not. Stathopoulos' politeness was worthy of note, as was his good taste in furniture and decoration. His living room was modern without resembling the operations room of the Starship *Enterprise*, as the houses of some of my wealthy clients do. I wondered who was responsible: Stathopoulos, Aliki or some expensive interior designer, one of those hired by people astute enough to know they lack taste.

During the whole of the forty-minute trip across town, from north-west to south, neither Stathopoulos nor the gunman whom he introduced as "Makis" had made a single mistake. There were no slip-ups when they ushered us from the basement garage to the living room, no opportunities for Drag and me to turn the tables. Makis had taken my gun, but where Stathopoulos was a watchful amateur, Makis struck me as being only semi-professional. Which didn't make him harmless – such types are trigger-happy.

But it meant that sooner or later he would make an error. And as soon as we got our chance I meant to make him and Stathopoulos curse the milk they sucked from their mother's tits.

"About life, I don't know, though you seem to be a man who already knows quite enough. About this particular case, however, you are missing a lot of important information, Mr Gazis."

There was that "Mr" again; both he and his wife liked addressing me formally.

"Which case do you mean?" I asked.

Drag and Makis stayed silent, one of them out of choice and the other because that was his job. Makis had put us in armchairs next to each other and sat himself opposite to watch our every move. He was still holding the Glock 40 he had introduced me to in the car, and pointed it at us. Drag was staring at Stathopoulos, who was sitting next to Makis, but I knew that all his attention was really focused on the gunman.

"Let's be frank, Mr Gazis. My wife has hired you to kill me. As for Mr Dragas, I know he has the reputation of being the best and most incorruptible officer in Athens, but I must confess that I don't know what part he plays in all this."

"Neither do I," Drag said, breaking his silence.

I tried to keep a straight face, but I couldn't help smiling.

"My feeling," said Stathopoulos, "is that as childhood friends, you cooperate with each other to the extent that you don't get under each other's feet. If I am mistaken, please correct me."

He was well informed, at any rate. Even Drag looked surprised for a second, but his grim expression quickly returned. When I'd asked him how stupid he could be and he had answered "very", I was talking about his failure to follow me without me noticing, but of course he was referring to his capture.

"My assumption is correct? Excellent. It's good for each of us to know how the other works," Stathopoulos continued, the smooth smile never slipping. "And on that score, you should know that Makis is here only as my bodyguard. I want you to listen to me, even if you have agreed to kill me."

"Can we have something to drink?" I asked to distract him.

He was probably telling the truth about not wanting to kill us, at least not immediately, or he wouldn't have brought us to his house. There are always places and gunmen for that kind of work. Still, I didn't feel at all comfortable with Makis' Glock staring me in the eyes. It was too ugly a companion. I just needed a bit of time.

Stathopoulos looked at Makis, who nodded me towards the bar. I got up, carefully. Maybe he was just there to stop his boss getting killed, but I couldn't be sure. Drag knew immediately what I was planning. The bar contained just about every drink imaginable. I poured myself a Johnnie Walker Blue Label – always choose the best, when it's for free. Even if it's going to waste.

"Can I get you one?" I asked Stathopoulos, raising my glass in a toast. I didn't wait for his reply. I threw the whisky in his face before Makis had a chance to turn his gun on me. Drag jumped up and headbutted Makis, who fell to the ground. I grabbed Stathopoulos and held a three-inch Gerber to his throat – luckily, Makis had missed it in the inside of my waistband when he searched me.

At school, Drag was the worst football player ever, when the ball was on the ground. His legs were so uncoordinated he couldn't dribble round a statue. But his head was phenomenal. Each time he took a header in the penalty area, his team members started celebrating even before the ball had gone in. Over the years his head had got hard enough to shatter breeze blocks. Which is why I almost felt sorry for Makis. Almost.

Everything happened in less than ten seconds, in silence. In a real fight, you don't often hear a groan. That's why I like the old noir films – the writers understood that when someone is battling for his life he hasn't even breath to waste.

I put my mouth close to Stathopoulos' ear.

"Now let's talk," I said.

He didn't seem perturbed. The smooth smile seemed even broader.

"I think I've found the right people to help me," he replied.

16

Makis had served in the Special Forces and had black belts in various martial arts. If Stathopoulos had been impressed by his qualifications, he was even more impressed by the way Drag dealt with him. Playing by the rules on soft mattresses bears little relation to real life. We laid Makis out on the sofa. I took back my gun and searched him for other weapons. Now we'd got things under control, I called Aliki. I was two hours late for our meeting, and her phone was off, but at least she didn't have to worry about being attacked by her husband, not while Drag and I were with him. The living room was full of photos of the two of them, from all over the world. Aliki was dazzling, especially in her wedding photo. Happy. *Different* from the Aliki I had met. Stathopoulos didn't look bad as a groom, either. I knew from Teri's gossip that the wedding had taken place on his fortieth birthday. He didn't look like he had aged a day. In one of the photos, he was lying on their bed, laughing, with his tie undone and his shirt unbuttoned, looking into the lens. In the large mirror behind him, Aliki's hair and her hand taking the picture were visible, but her other hand was covering her exquisite face.

Seeing me staring, Stathopoulos said, "We got married three years ago, after we'd known each other only a month. Until then I'd never had a lasting relationship. Every woman I'd met ended up getting on my nerves over stupid little things. With Aliki even that first month was unnecessary; I knew she was the one right from the beginning, since her first breath beside me. Have you ever been in love like that, Mr Gazis? Mr Dragas?"

I wasn't about to explain that it had happened to us, with the same woman. Drag and I didn't talk about it. For us, best friends know when *not* to discuss something.

Getting no response, Stathopoulos continued, "It was her dream, to go to Cuba. That's where we spent our honeymoon. Do you know how marvellous it feels to realize a dream for the person you've dreamt about? I didn't. I discovered it then for the first time. But that wasn't all that I discovered…"

He paused and sighed. As if he had to summon up courage for what he was about to say.

"That was when I first saw the blood."

Another pause. Another sigh. His voice even broke as he spoke. He was either a brilliant actor, or genuinely moved.

"Aliki likes… has a habit of… she cuts herself… self-mutilation. When you met her in La Luna I'm sure that she either showed you her scars or promised to. The scars she claims I gave her, by hitting or cutting her or whatever. Am I right?"

Drag glanced at me. I said nothing. I looked again at the photo. Something about it seemed strange to me, but I couldn't put my finger on it. Stathopoulos had probably never met with such a lack of response to one of his courtroom speeches.

"I confess that I was a very jealous husband at the beginning. How could I not be? You've seen what she looks like, and she enjoys having men drooling over her. I've done some things I'm not proud of... shouted at her... got angry... frightened her. Over trifles, I know. Blind jealousy, when all she did was a bit of harmless flirting. But that's how it is – when you're already forty and you've never felt this... this crazy about someone and you can't stand the idea that she might leave you, you lose it... you totally lose it. Because you know you're not going to get another shot at crazy love like that again. Either you keep hold of it or you're finished. I felt ready to die... and... to kill... Even a few months after the Cuba incident, when I thought she had got over it, we had a stupid fight, a big one, when I saw her laughing too much at an actor's jokes... Until she started to cut herself again, with anything she could get her hands on. That put an end to my madness – her sickness healed mine. The only thing I could think of was to help her recover. I've taken her to the top psychiatrists in Greece, England and Switzerland... Always the same story... At the beginning she tells them what she probably told you – that I do these things to her body but not the face to make it look like an accident – but, after a few sessions she ends up in tears, saying that I'm her only love and she hates me for loving her so much because she doesn't deserve it, which is why she wants to get back at me."

"She hates you enough to want to kill you?" I asked.

"That's what she said to one psychiatrist. That only when I'm dead will she feel free to kill herself, as she wants."

"I thought psychiatrists were sworn to confidentiality," Drag said.

"Not exactly, Mr Dragas. Not if I pay them to tell me what she says. But it turns out that I needn't have purchased this particular piece of information. Three months ago, she took an overdose. I came back from work and found her there in the living room, covered in vomit, and rushed her to hospital. It was her vomiting that saved her – otherwise, the stomach pump wouldn't have been enough. When she opened her eyes and realized that she was still alive the first thing she told me was that she was going to kill me for not letting her die."

I thought of Aliki Stylianou at the restaurant. Bright, enticing, a goddess… Stathopoulos seemed to be describing a completely different person. I thought of her waiting for me, at the meeting place she'd arranged earlier. Feeling lonely and frightened, not knowing what was going on. Could the picture I had of her be so wrong? It wouldn't have been the first time. The older you get, the more you can be sure of just one thing: you'll never really understand people.

"I let her choose her own therapist after that. Antonis Rizos is his name. She seemed to have made some progress with him, seemed healthier these past couple of months, met him quite often. Maybe too often. And I didn't interfere, didn't want him to tell her – I checked him out; he's a leftist, an idealist, all about not doing his job for the money. Wasn't sure if I could bribe him. But after what happened yesterday, I'll pay him a visit to find out what he knows."

Planning his next move, already. As if he had nothing to fear, after the stunt he pulled on us. Maybe he thought Drag's presence would keep him safe from me. Maybe he wasn't totally wrong.

"Perhaps you think I'm just telling you all this to stop you from killing me?" Stathopoulos asked, at last.

"The idea did cross my mind," I said.

I hadn't yet received a penny to take care of him but when someone puts a gun to my head I'm prepared to waive my principles and take care of him for free.

"I'm telling you because I want to employ you, Mr Gazis. And you too, Mr Dragas, if you work together."

"We don't work together and I'm not for hire," Drag said, curtly.

The second half was true.

"Employ me to do what?" I asked, since I *was* for hire.

Even when someone has stuck a gun in my face, I feel obliged to examine every professional proposition carefully, wherever it comes from.

"Yesterday, the murderers of the girl..."

"Elsa Dalla?"

However good Drag is at his work, he can't rid himself of that habit all cops have of asking obvious questions to get obvious answers.

"Yes. It wasn't her they were after. They thought they'd killed Aliki."

"And how would you happen to know that, Mr Stathopoulos?" Drag asked.

It seemed ridiculous to me that after all that had happened, they kept calling each other "Mr". Maybe they were more polite than I was.

"Because it wasn't their first attempt to murder Aliki. They've tried twice before."

He described both attempts, in exactly the same way as Aliki had described them to me.

"Both times Aliki had miraculous escapes but she persuaded herself that they were just accidents, refusing to accept that she had been the target."

That's what she told you, I thought.

"Why should she do that?" Drag asked.

"I don't know. The police got nowhere with the faulty brake, and the motorcyclist – a Bulgarian – skidded on some spilt oil, just missed Aliki and slammed into a lorry. No papers. Security had nothing on him."

"Who would want to kill her?"

"I don't know that, either. Enquiries into the identity of the motorcyclist drew a blank. The bike was stolen and he had nothing except a shopping list in Bulgarian. No fingerprints in the system, the Bulgarian police couldn't help... You can check the archive, Mr Dragas. Aliki only has friends; I can't think of anyone who has a grudge against her. I have hired so many people to look into it since that first attempt and they've come up with nothing. Nothing at all."

"From what you've told us, they could just wait for Aliki to make a good job of it on her own," Drag said.

However long I've known him, I still can't fathom how Drag comes out with such things. Discretion is one of the few virtues he lacks. He never beats about the bush, says just what's on his mind regardless of the audience and the circumstances. Stathopoulos looked at him coldly, but didn't say anything. He needed us – if he was to be believed.

"Why was Dalla in Aliki's BMW?" Drag asked.

"I don't know."

"Her earlier relationships?" I said.

"What do you mean?"

"A connection with someone from her past life?"

"I don't think so. I don't… know. When the first attempt happened we'd already been married two years. Is it possible? Wouldn't they have acted sooner? Who would wait so long to get revenge?"

For a lawyer he seemed quite ignorant of how long people can nurse a desire for revenge. Or that's how he wanted it to appear.

"Do you know the people she dated?" Drag demanded. "I mean, before you got married. Let's say, going back to a couple of years before you met."

"I don't know anything about her love life before I met her. It doesn't concern me."

Nothing, except for that little video with the banker Aliki had told me about. I didn't say anything. I hadn't even mentioned it to Drag – call it professional confidentiality.

"Why doesn't it concern you?" Drag insisted.

"I'm only concerned with information I can use. The names of my wife's former boyfriends would merely make me feel uncomfortable if I should meet them. At worst, I would start imagining her in bed with them. I'd rather not know. I explained it all to Aliki when we decided to get married but she saw things differently. She insisted I had to be open about my past and write down the names of all my former lovers. I continued to believe in the power of ignorance, and learnt nothing at all about hers."

"Why the jealousy, then?"

"I told you that my jealousy didn't last long. And it was a jealousy about the present, not the shadows of the past."

As Drag didn't say anything, I stepped in.

"From what you say about the murder attempts, you need a bodyguard for your wife. Which I am not."

"I don't want you for anything like that. I've got Makis for a bodyguard."

I glanced at the still-unconscious body stretched out on the sofa. Three murder attempts by guys who may, or may not, have been joking. He wasn't much good even as a bodyguard.

"The reason I want to employ you, Mr Gazis, is that I no longer have any faith in the people I've been paying to help me with this case. I don't think they're up to it, whereas you, I've heard, are the best – which my recent experience bears out."

He paused. Aliki's voice echoed in my mind: "I'm scared, really scared… they killed that girl… thought it was me… he killed her." If I was certain Stathopoulos was the one trying to kill Aliki, I'd have no problem killing him myself, when Drag wasn't around. But I wasn't so sure any more as to the wrongs and rights of the case. Aliki wanted me to kill someone who was prepared to pay me to save her. Something about the story felt wrong. Plus, I hadn't been paid yet.

"I will pay you whatever sum of money. *Whatever*," Stathopoulos said. "You name it. I mean it, Mr Gazis. I want you to find out who is trying to kill her. If you can also discover *why*, that's even better. I will pay whatever you ask to find him and take care of him."

Nobody ever said the life of a conscientious caretaker was easy. It could, however, be quite profitable.

17

Apart from my three close friends, people who know me either want to employ me, or are my victims. I wondered which of my former employers had told Stathopoulos about me. Whoever it was knew about Drag as well, which made the list of candidates shorter. But Stathopoulos refused to tell me. He just said he'd started making enquiries when Makis showed him a photo he'd taken of Aliki and me from a hiding place in the restaurant's kitchen. Maybe he wasn't altogether useless. I'd asked Stathopoulos for a couple of days to think about his proposition. To help me think, he had opened up his safe and given me sixty 500-euro notes. Thirty thousand. No need to return them, he said, if I were to refuse. It was payment for my thinking time. Or a down payment, if I accepted. He didn't stop there. Immediately after, he took out his chequebook, wrote a cheque and put it in my pocket. The amount was blank. If my thoughts led me to undertake the case, he said, I could put in any sum I liked and he would sign it. Any sum, he stressed again. I told him that I didn't take cheques; if I undertook the case he would have to deposit the required amount in an account in Zurich. He insisted that I take it, as a sign of his goodwill. Then he went on to give Drag the names of all the private detectives he had hired to investigate the attempts on Aliki's life. He even tied up the Rottweiler that was his most effective security guard. As we left, he told us he wasn't too worried about Aliki – she had phoned him the day before to tell him that she was alright but in hiding after what had happened. He tried to trace her call, but got nowhere. At least one of them was lying. Maybe they both were. I had started to doubt anything said by anyone involved in this case.

I kept on trying to phone Aliki. I was a professional, and I owed her that much. But she didn't answer, which meant I still couldn't be sure who I was supposed to kill.

18

Maria came down to bring me the morning papers. I like to hold the paper in my hands, to smell the ink, even if it makes me look like a time traveller from the Stone Age. On the screen, the newspaper is weightless, like most of the stories that morons make up in the hope it will become viral.

As Maria descended the stairs, the sensors were activated one by one, flashing in lights above my door. I wanted to know exactly where my visitors were at any one time, in case they were uninvited. Aliki, Elsa and the BMW were spread across all the front pages. The journalists were in full cry and Drag had been named as the officer in charge of the investigation. He and I would have to be even more careful about meeting in public.

I was discussing this with Maria when she touched me. We have an unwritten, unspoken rule. I never touch her first. It only happens when she wants to. At first everything was perfect between her and Sotiris – his wheelchair seemed invisible. But as his multiple sclerosis started to take hold, the wheelchair became a fixture in the background. Not that it's ever become an issue – they love each other too much to let it.

The only thing they're missing, the one that his illness has robbed them of, she looks for in me, though much less frequently than I'd like her to. She knows that she can rely on me, and that I'd never create a problem for her and Sotiris who, I suspect, knows what's going on. I don't ask Maria because it's none of my business. And neither Drag nor Teri knows anything about our encounters, Drag for obvious reasons and Teri because she doesn't think there's a problem. The last time we discussed the subject, before Maria had even met Sotiris, Teri said to me: "Stratos, can I ask you something?"

"Ask away."

"Aren't you in love with Maria?"

"Yes."

"But she's also in love with Drag."

"Yes."

"Who you also love."

"Mmm."

"And he loves you."

"I believe so."

"So you love each other in a circle."

"I never thought about it like that, but… yes."

"Why don't you live together?"

"Who?"

"All of you – it would be more convenient for me than having to visit each of you separately."

"We should live together to make your life easier. That's what you're proposing?"

"To make things easier for *yourselves*."

"In what way?"

"You'd be together."

"All of us?"

"Yep. You with Maria, Maria with Drag, Drag with you – OK, you and him will just be friends, though believe me, you don't know what you're missing… If you live together, the three of you, you'll rid yourselves of all those hang-ups that take up so much of your time, and you won't have to worry about hiding who you love from each other."

"According to your logic, since all of us love you…"

"At last! I thought you were never going to ask. Where should we stay? This is going to be so great! The four of us will get on brilliantly. And if it bothers you I won't bring many customers home, just those who don't moan too much."

The idea of having just one partner had never been part of Teri's world view, until she recently fell in love herself.

When we make love Maria never makes loud noises. My flat is soundproofed anyway, but I think she feels that her voice would somehow validate what we are doing, while silence would allow it to go unnoticed. She doesn't make loud noises but she often quietly cries; from the moment we lie naked in bed she cries and pulls me closer to her and I don't say anything, I just hold her tighter and make love to her with a passion I hope will silence her or make her tears flow forever when she's in my arms.

When we'd finished, Maria stroked my nose.

"How many times have you broken it?"

"Many."

The last person who'd broken it was Linesman. He got his nickname from waving a flag on the sidelines of local football games – that was his hobby. He had a body like his idol Dolph Lundgren and worked as muscle for whoever hired him. Drag told me Linesman attended meetings of the neo-Nazi Golden Dawn party, who wanted to rid Greece of all immigrants. Their supporters regularly attacked Middle Eastern and African street traders, wherever they tried to sell their goods. Linesman was probably paid for terrorizing the immigrants – the party came third in the recent elections and was funded handsomely from the federal budget.

Linesman and I had a relationship of mutual respect, until I woke up in an empty warehouse, tied to a chair, and Linesman kicked me in the head. "Don't take it personally, it's just work," he said, and proceeded to give me a good beating with his fists as well as chains. He'd been hired by the owner of a club whose brother I had taken care of. The brother was a coke addict who took underage whores to his house and killed them after having cut up their faces. One of the very rare cases I had worked on for free. "Word on the street is you're the best," Linesman said. "But if you were really the best, would you be here?"

He'd waylaid me earlier that evening, at an old stone-built coffee house in Chalandri belonging to someone I knew. For years the place had been in a state of deadlocked antagonism with the high-class boutique that had opened next door, the outcome of which would determine the character of the neighbourhood. Then the crisis came, the boutique evaporated in no time and I became a regular, smitten with the shop's fantastic Greek coffee. So many coffee houses around me in Psychiko and I had to make the half-hour journey to and from Chalandri. Linesman ambushed me – the owner had let him hide behind the bar and made sure I sat with my back turned to him.

"It's a good thing you aren't enjoying it," I told him after I had stopped spitting blood, during one of his rest breaks.

Breaks were necessary, he told me, because he still had a lot left to do to me while waiting for his employer to turn up to witness me being killed. Burnt alive, to be exact. This delay was what saved me. "It's a good thing because…," I continued, diverting his attention just enough for Drag to burst into the warehouse through the window, shattering the glass and rolling to one side to avoid becoming an easy target. Linesman had nothing on him, besides the chains. His gun was on the table, out of his immediate reach, which was why he went straight for Drag, his chains raised ready to strike. Drag shot him twice in the chest, but it didn't seem to have any effect. Drag is the coolest customer I know, but when he saw Linesman take a third bullet without collapsing, he frowned and shot him in the head. That stopped him for good.

"Could you just tell me what you were doing all that time outside?" I asked Drag.

"I needed to work out the right angle of collision with the window," he answered earnestly. Drag the geometry expert.

Maria didn't know about Linesman or about the killings of his employer and the coffee shop owner that I carried out later that night. She also didn't know – because she doesn't need to worry more than she already does – that a couple of weeks after that night Drag found out from one of his informants that Linesman's lover was looking for those responsible for his death. We never heard from her or anyone she hired, and we didn't lose any sleep over it. Our line of work gives us so many things to be concerned about that we can't be bothered with threats from unknown amateurs.

However, in order to help her worry less, I told Maria about Drag's newest gadget, the pea-sized transmitter, which fitted under the sole without you even feeling it. It was that transmitter that had saved my life. What made it extremely useful was that if it received pressure in a particular sequence of shorter and longer duration it sent an SOS to a prearranged list of recipients. Drag's list and mine were as short as it got, comprising just us two.

"I saw Drag on the news. A photo, that is. They said that he was in charge of the case," Maria said, after getting dressed.

"Mmm."

I never know what to do when she mentions Drag's name, so I speak even less than usual.

"He's their top man," she said.

"He's good. Really good."

"His raincoat looked awful, though."

"Mmm."

"Seems like he has no one to look after him."

I kept looking at her. I never mentioned anything to Drag about Maria and Sotiris' life together and nothing to Maria about Drag's love life – not that there was anything to say. That was my silent agreement with the two of them.

"Tell him."

"Tell him what?"

"To find someone to look after him."

I didn't know what to say. I just nodded.

"Say it's your own idea. Don't mention me."

I nodded again.

"Tell him."

I poured her a coffee. Neither of us spoke for a while.

"How are things going with the case? Are you getting anywhere?"

I wanted to tell her that at that moment, having just made love, I couldn't care less if we were getting anywhere. Neither could I care if Aliki Stylianou was being mistreated by her bastard husband or if she was a crazy fantasist. I didn't care about the money or about the corpse of Elsa Dalla, whose open eyes seemed to be full of questions. What mattered was that I was with Maria. What mattered was the next time she came down to my room. Touched me. Showed that she wanted me.

Instead, I said: "Drag will sort it all out in the end. For sure. Always does."

"What about you?"

"I hope that I'll sort it out myself, and that I'll do it just before he starts arresting people, so that I can earn my wage and pay the rent. You have no idea what a bad lot my landlady is. She doesn't like me one bit; if I don't pay her on time she'll chuck me out."

"I, on the other hand, think you've won her over. Years ago."

Saying that, she kissed me on the cheek and stroked my eyes before leaving. Sometimes you watch the door closing, the same door you've seen close thousands of times, and suddenly something gets so tight inside you that you suspect you might still have a heart.

19

"I need to see you."

Aliki. Calling from a payphone. Her voice low and even more frightened this time.

It was 4.30 in the morning but she didn't interrupt my sleep – I don't sleep easily after spending time with Maria.

"Where are you?"

She gave me the address of a fast-food joint in Zografou. I told her I'd be there in fifteen minutes. Made it in ten. It was on the ground floor of one of the gazillion apartment buildings in the area, many of them new and costing twice as much as those in similar districts in Athens. Tens of thousands of students vying for a rental near the university. Demand. Keeps the market going, never mind the crisis.

A young couple were making out in a corner of the shop, minding their own business. They were the only customers apart from Aliki. She sat at a table near the side entrance, huddled over her mobile, a beanie on her head. She looked pale, and even more beautiful without make-up, the azure of her eyes heightened by the dark circles that clouded them. I thought of her husband, when they first got married. When they were still in love, or believed they were. I imagined what it would be like to have this woman in bed with you. I imagined him thinking that he might lose her, that he might never kiss those dimples again.

"You're here," she said and grabbed my hand.

Her fingers were cold and trembling. She was still wearing the same clothes as the last time I saw her.

"Couldn't make it yesterday – I had a run-in with your husband."

"You did? And?"

She sounded hopeful. Looked it, too. If I was still standing, maybe I had already delivered?

"And nothing, yet. What happened the other night, with your car? How was that girl...?"

But she wasn't listening – pulled her hand from mine.

"He tried to win you over, didn't he? Told you it's all my imagination."

"On the contrary, he very much believes you're in danger."

"Yes, from him!"

"He says not. He wants to hire me to protect you."

She laughed, then grew angry.

"And you fell for that? How much did he offer you to betray me?"

To betray her. She seemed to have blocked out the fact that I wasn't hers to begin with.

"I want to help you. But I haven't agreed to anything with you, or him, yet. Tell me what happened with Elsa Dalla – how come she was driving your car?"

Her incredible eyes suddenly widened.

"You bastard, you brought them here!" she said.

I followed her gaze and saw Makis burst through the front entrance. She leapt over her chair and ran out of the side door. Makis started towards her, but saw me get up and stopped. He may have thought of pushing past me but decided against it, running back the way he'd come in. When I went out, Aliki had vanished, as I'd expected. Makis was looking left and right, trying to decide which way to give chase. If he were smarter, he would have driven round the block to see if he could catch her running. That's what I did. I went round and round, while trying to get her on the phone. I couldn't spot her anywhere and her phone was switched off. Makis, too, was gone, as if the darkness in the street had swallowed them both. Half an hour later I was back at the fast-food joint, in case she'd left anything that might help me find her. The guy behind the counter was half-asleep and useless. It would have been good if Makis were still around. I'd make him tell me how he found us. While driving to Zografou I'd made sure that no one was following me, so how did he know where Aliki was? I could drop by my new friend Vassilis and ask him and Makis both. Although I'd probably have to hear Vassilis' stock response that he was concerned about her and wanted to make sure she was safe. I had just sent Aliki a text to reassure her I had nothing to do with Makis' appearance, when someone behind me said: "You're Stratos, right?"

I turned to see a good-looking guy, athletic, with a face that reminded me of Richard Gere in his youth, when all the women were drooling over him. About forty, blond, blue-eyed, with wrinkles that worked in his favour, and a rather large nose – one of those that don't often work on women but make men seem more striking.

"Do we know each other?" I said.

"I'm Nikos. Nikos Zois," he said, "Teri's boyfriend."

He held out his hand and smiled broadly. Although Teri referred to him as her "hunk", I'd put that down to her incurable tendency to exaggerate. But even though he was at least three inches shorter than me, he had presence. And a handshake that was firm and warm.

"I've seen you in photos with Teri. I live round the corner, and was working late, so I thought I'd grab a double pita souvlaki – will you join me?"

I wanted to find Aliki and work out whether she, or her husband, was telling the truth. But it was 5.30 in the morning, I had no idea where she was and my text hadn't reached her, so my mobile service informed me. The possibility of sharing a couple of souvlakia with my transsexual friend's boyfriend suddenly made a lot of sense.

"I never say no to souvlaki," I told him.

"So, I hear you've got a toy factory?" I asked Nikos after he returned with our double pitas, fried potatoes, Greek salad and beers – he had insisted on paying for everything.

"I wouldn't exactly call it a factory," he said, grabbing a colossal bite from his chicken souvlaki with yoghurt. I had opted for pork with tzatziki, following my rule that when you dive into cholesterol you need to go all the way.

"Teri mentioned you're modest about it," I said.

She'd called it a whacking big thing making board games, construction toys, masks, electronic games and probably a few other things I couldn't remember.

"A lot of the stuff we sell we just import; we don't make everything ourselves. But we do produce a fair amount."

"And you started with quite a small workshop."

"I see that Reuters have released everything," he said, smiling.

"Maybe we should give her a call, to come and join us," I suggested.

"No, no, she… is asleep now. We… we were together earlier," he said, almost shyly.

"Ah," I said.

"Yes. I actually can't sleep easily after spending time with her. So I thought I'd get some work done, get through the unanswered emails. And have some of my favourite souvlaki."

I nodded, tasted the potatoes. Pre-fried ones, as in most fast-food joints, but still tasty. It was the first time I'd heard someone who echoed my feelings about Maria.

"I love their souvlaki. Seems like every shop around is closing to become an eatery or cafeteria, but most are trying to make easy money. This one never disappoints. So, she's been talking about me a lot?" he asked, like a teenager wanting confirmation that his love interest is equally returned.

"She's proud of your success," I replied.

"Although being proud and being in love are hardly the same thing," he said.

He seemed to really want that confirmation, which I found amusing and pleasing at the same time. Amusing because he was too old to act like an adolescent. Pleasing because Teri hadn't exactly been lucky in love in the past. Neither her profession, nor her change of gender had been of much help.

"I don't think they contradict each other, either," I told him.

He studied me for a bit, with an inquisitive smile.

"You don't give too much away, do you?" he finally said.

"Teri told me you met by chance," I said, instead of responding.

"Yes, I was – I *am* – a new volunteer at the centre, I first saw her there."

Teri had been volunteering for a non-governmental organization helping abused children. It was one of the NGOs that actually did what they claimed to do, instead of embezzling federal money. And she was doing tons of work, at their child abuse prevention centre. Apparently, domestic violence had grown rapidly with the crisis, and children were easy targets. Teri had declared her profession as "beautician" at the NGO and hadn't told anyone about being transsexual. Nobody had asked. They accepted her as a woman, which wasn't surprising given how few male characteristics she ever had.

"She is truly fantastic, you know – I mean, you are best friends, so of course you know – but she is," he said.

"According to Teri you've helped a lot, too, donated loads of toys."

"That was nothing. The toys were there, we put them in a truck – no effort. What she does for these kids, how she's there for everything they need, when they have nightmares and need a hug or when they want to play and she organizes all kinds of fun things to do…"

He was proud of her too. Which was great, but made it hard for me to ask him what I really wanted to know. Which was how he felt about her being transgender and, most importantly, if he didn't mind her being a sex worker. Sharing your beloved with the rest of the world couldn't be as wonderful as everything else he was describing.

"And you, Stratos, you too are a businessman, right?" he asked.

"I try to be, with all that's going on," I said.

Teri had told me that when Nikos had asked her about me she had been as vague as possible, mentioning that I was doing something incomprehensible to her, software-related.

"What exactly do you work on, if you don't mind me asking?"

I didn't mind. I had my story at the ready, had used it before.

"Selling software packages for teams in various sports, to help them monitor their performance."

I'd learnt a bit about that stuff from a former client. Enough to be able to bullshit about it.

"Nice! Many clients?"

"Not too many, these days."

"You're expensive?"

"You could say that."

"So what's your plan, for the immediate future?"

That was a damn good question. I didn't yet have much of an answer.

20

It was a quarter to ten in the morning when I called Drag. I told him I was in my car, outside Antonis Rizos' practice, but the therapist hadn't appeared yet. I knew what he looked like from his sparse website, containing only his photo, contact details and office hours. Which he didn't seem too keen to keep.

I spared Drag the details of my meeting with Nikos Zois. I assumed that, with the pressure he was under to find Elsa Dalla's murderer and where Aliki was, details about Teri's love life were not high on his list of interests. Drag informed me that he already had someone tailing Vassilis around the clock, to report on his every move. Drag expected him to visit Rizos, as he'd told us he would, but Vassilis had left his house earlier that morning to go straight to the Courthouse at the former Army Cadet School. A day like any other, for the working lawyer. His wife missing, a murder in her car, and he was at his post, cross-examining witnesses for one of his cases. Drag had a second guy stationed at Vassilis' house, to keep tabs on Makis in case he and Vassilis had left separately. The second cop reported to Drag that Makis hadn't left the house at all the previous day. The quality of the Greek police force never ceases to amaze me. But I couldn't give Drag my honest opinion, because I'd then have to reveal that I'd seen Makis when I met Aliki the previous night, something I also hadn't mentioned to Drag.

"I called Rizos myself, today. He didn't pick up," Drag said.

"OK. Let me know if anything else comes up," I told him.

"Of course, master. Always at your service," he said, and I would have smiled but I hung up as Antonis Rizos had just appeared around the corner, walking towards his office. He wasn't alone. Makis was walking beside him.

21

I let them enter the apartment building where Rizos had his penthouse practice, before I got out of the car and ran to the main entrance. It was unlocked, as it had been earlier. I took the stairs, keeping my eyes on the elevator to see if anyone used it. I reached the third floor a few seconds later, and tried the door to his practice. It was locked. I knew that some doctors keep apartments in the same building as their practices, to make their lives easier. But I had checked the names on the doorbells, and Rizos' name was only on one. That didn't make it certain that Rizos and Makis were behind the locked door – but it made it highly probable. There was no other apartment on the third floor, no immediate neighbours to worry about. I put my ear to the door, waited for a while. I heard some subdued conversation, but I couldn't make out the words. They were either far from the door or trying to make sure no one could hear them. Maybe they were planning to overthrow the government – Rizos had signed all sorts of web petitions calling for action against the third memorandum with the EU and those who enforced its draconian financial measures. And Makis was obviously a deep political thinker.

I knocked on the door and stepped to the side. No response. Maybe Makis was having a therapy session to overcome the shame at the way we'd jumped him the other night. I knocked again, harder this time, and shouted: "courier for Dr Rizos". I checked the peephole in the door. I was sure Makis would peer through it to see who it was. I saw movement behind the peephole and kicked the door near the keyhole, which is usually the weakest part. I heard the guy behind the door grunt, as it fell on him. It was Rizos. Makis was kneeling behind him, with his gun out. He may have been stupid but at least he'd sent Rizos to the door, to be on the safe side. He took aim at me and missed, as I ducked and dropped to the floor out of his line of vision. His gunshot had been as loud as a cannon and I heard doors being opened downstairs. People trying to find out what was going on, probably calling the police already.

"Show yourself, you fucking fucker," Makis shouted, exposing his impressive vocabulary.

What was happening made little sense to me. Makis may have hated my guts but his employer claimed to want to hire me. His orders couldn't be to shoot me at first sight. And Makis had kept his distance from me at the fast-food joint. What had changed? If I managed to get Rizos out of there and neutralized Makis, I would probably have the chance to find out. From the doorway I saw Rizos moving, trying to get the doorframe off him. I had to do something fast, before the cops arrived.

"Come on, you fucker," Makis repeated.

I kept looking at Rizos. He seemed at a loss, but he met my gaze. I gestured to him to roll over towards me. It was a gamble, if Makis took another shot at him, but I was willing to bet that his full attention would be on the door, waiting for me to appear. Also, by rolling over, Rizos had a better chance of not being hit, and the doorframe might possibly protect him.

"Come on, chickenshit, show your face, come on, come on," Makis kept ranting, the pitch of his voice rising.

Rizos rolled over very quickly for a man of his age – he looked like he was in his late sixties, but he was thin and muscular, he probably worked out. Makis didn't try to shoot him. He just said "What the fuck?"

"This way," I shouted to Rizos from the hallway, loud enough for Makis to hear me. Makis appeared in the doorway soon enough, and looked around. I stepped out of the window recess where I was hiding and knocked him cold, just as the first police sirens made themselves heard.

22

"Who *are* you?" Antonis Rizos asked me.

We were in my car, several blocks away from his office. He had agreed to come with me, as he said he didn't feel like talking to the "fucking cops" until he calmed down. Consistent with his leftist background, rather than an echo of Makis' vocabulary.

"That's not important."

"It is to me. I want to know who saved me."

"So he wanted to kill you?"

"Your name, first."

His hair was just now greying at the temples but his face was no longer youthful. Still, he had a certain energy, now he had regained his composure.

"Stratos."

"Stratos…"

"That's all I'll give you."

"And what were you doing in my office?"

"I wanted to ask you a few questions about Aliki Stylianou."

"You, too."

I nodded.

"Why are you interested?"

"I think she's in danger. I want to help her."

"Why?" he insisted with the questions. Probably the therapist in him.

"I like righting wrongs," I told him, although that wasn't necessarily true.

He stared at me, as if trying to find out if I was sincere.

"Tell me what happened with Makis," I said.

"He approached me outside my office, said he'd like to book an appointment, that he had some personal issues. I asked him to call to arrange one, but he said he'd been having suicidal thoughts daily and if I could see him right now he would appreciate it."

"So you told him to come upstairs?"

"Yes. He didn't strike me as the suicidal type, the way he talked and behaved, but I've seen so much counter-intuitive stuff happen, that..."

"And he attacked you?"

"Locked the door and pulled a gun on me as soon as we were in the office."

"Because...?"

"He said he wanted to know everything Aliki had told me and where he could find her. Of course I have no idea where she is, and I'd never reveal confidential information."

"Not even at gunpoint?"

"I'm an old commie, Stratos, and proud of it. I've been in more protests and street fights than I care to remember. Violence doesn't intimidate me."

Makis wanted to know where Aliki was and what Rizos knew. Both questions Vassilis would have sent Makis to find answers to, but why didn't Makis at least try to get the information before he resorted to violence? It could be that he liked it, but he was a hired gun. He should follow Vassilis' orders. Once again, as in his shooting at me, his actions seemed incomprehensible.

"Did he tell you that he worked for her husband?" I asked him.

"He did."

"So he wanted to know if you knew about him torturing her."

"I can't comment on that."

"If she confided in you…"

"I won't tell you anything that was discussed in her sessions."

"Even if it is to help her stay alive?"

"I know you probably saved my life today. But I don't know what your intentions towards Aliki are, and even if I knew that you are on her side, I still wouldn't tell you."

On her side. So there was another side, and that could only be Vassilis. I believed Rizos that he wouldn't tell me anything specific, even if I tried to beat it out of him, and I felt that he had had enough violence for one day. I tried another approach.

"Aren't you required by law, however, to report domestic abuse cases? So if something like that was happening, wouldn't you…?"

"Let me put it this way," he interrupted me. "Laws are often rubbish. Laws dealing with something as fragile as the mental state and feelings of humans are always rubbish, because each case is different from the next. And no, if I didn't think that a patient would gain by my reporting hypothetical abuse, I wouldn't report it. In my practice, I make the laws."

He was very carefully informing me that everything that Aliki had said was true.

"Did you know Elsa Dalla, the murdered woman in Aliki's car?" I asked him.

"Never heard of her, until I saw the news."

A long pause followed. Which he broke. "However, I must say…"

"Yes?"

"I am under the impression, based on his behaviour, that this guy, Makis, has a strong personal interest in the case. Thank you for your help, I need to walk a bit now," he said, and got out of my car.

23

Leaving Rizos' neighbourhood, I had two options. The first was to drive straight to the Courthouse, grab Vassilis and make him tell me what was going on with Makis – if he knew, that is. Rizos' suggestion that Makis might have a personal interest in the case was still swirling around my brain. Maybe I could beat a confession out of Vassilis that, after all, he did want to kill Aliki or have her imprisoned in his house, away from other men's eyes. Or maybe I wouldn't get anything and I would look like a big intimidating fool. Also, the fact that the Courthouse area was filled with cops and my face was all over the media meant that showing up there was probably not the brightest idea. I would have to see Vassilis later. I called Drag, told him what had happened at Rizos' office and asked him to make Makis talk.

"Thank you so much for this advice. I would never have thought of it myself," Drag replied. The case was probably starting to get on his nerves, just a bit.

The second option was to talk to Teri. I loved spending time with her, either in person or on the phone, because talking to childhood friends always makes you feel happy. In this case I had one more reason to talk to her, because she knew something no one else did: the identity of Aliki's close female friend. I intended to talk to her before telling Drag. Plenty of people just clam up in the presence of a cop. If, however, someone other than a cop goes to have an unofficial chat with them, there's a good chance they'll open up. Especially if that person is highly recommended for his discretion, as I am. Aliki's friend had first contacted Teri, looking for a caretaker. Drag didn't know about this. He thought that Aliki had communicated directly with Teri, and there was no reason for me to correct him. All I knew about the friend was that her first name was Lena, which Aliki had told me at the restaurant. To find out more, I called Teri. She decided to play hard to get.

"So, you want to find out who and where she is?"

"Yes. Drag and I are getting nowhere. We have to find somebody with some answers."

"Answers... mmm..."

"So... you going to tell me?"

"Of course."

"I'm listening."

"I'll tell you if you come to my place. I've prepared my world-class lamb espetadas and I want to have someone to share them with, but no one's around. Maria spends all day, every day with Sotiris, you're tearing around all the time with Drag..."

She really enjoyed calling the recipe "lamb espetadas", although it was basically lamb steaks grilled on skewers with some bay leaves on top. She thought it made the food sound more exotic.

"It's only been two weeks since we last got together..." I said.

"Two weeks? You're talking about someone you love. Someone who hates to be on their own."

"I thought you had Nikos."

"But who do I have to talk to *about* Nikos? Get your arse over here, right now. And tell that big dope Drag to speak to me soon or else…"

"Or else, what?"

"Just tell him 'Or else…' That's what they say in the movies. If he doesn't, I'll put on my pink tights and my mauve shawl, no bra, and I'll come and pay him a visit at Security Headquarters in front of all those cops, just to embarrass him."

"Teri, we're under a lot of pressure here, we really have to…"

"*I* really have to talk to you. Need to talk to you. I've so much to tell you about Nikos… If I don't tell you, then who will I tell? Have you ever heard me say that I'm in love before?"

"Several dozen times."

Of course, all of her former infatuations had been with clients who had gradually become lovers. Nikos Zois was the first in many years that she had met outside her bed and taken into it.

"Those were just passing fancies. This is the real thing."

"Teri, please, I need…"

"Pop in for a chat, just a chat! Nikos may come by later and you can meet him… These are my terms. Come by and I'll tell you what you want to know."

"I actually met him last night."

"What? Is this a joke? No, it's not a joke, because you'd never joke about something like that, oh my God, when?

Last night, how? After… No, don't tell me, be here in five and then tell me everything."

"Look…"

"In five!"

She hung up the phone.

Teri lives in a spacious old two-storey house in Galatsi, with views of the Veikou Wood from its balconies. An inheritance from her grandmother who stoutly maintained that Galatsi was, traditionally, the most aristocratic district of Athens, haughtily dismissing the theory that it got its name from the shepherds who roamed the area in the eighteenth century, shouting "milk: gala, gala, galataki". Her proud grandmother had been delighted to hear that her first grandchild was a boy. Luckily for everyone she quickly changed her will and left him the house, then died before Teri reached adolescence. Lucky Grandma. Even luckier Teri. Or maybe not so lucky with the ENFIA taxation on everybody that dares own a house.

I knocked on the door and the moment she opened it she threw me on her sofa – or at least tried to.

"You should really lose some weight. I can't beat you now like I used to," she said.

"When?"

"Shut up. Tell me everything. Where, when, how, why did you meet? What did he tell you?"

"If I shut up how can I tell you everything?"

"You're the muscle, you aren't allowed to be funny. Speak!"

I told her everything. Including how proud he seemed of her. Teri just stood there, smiling like an idiot.

"So?" I said.

"I'm over the moon. Outrageously, ridiculously happy. I want to turn back-flips in the air, do Comăneci's Olympic jump '76."

"You're old enough to remember that?"

"Yes, yes, fuck you too. I want time to freeze so that we stay exactly as we are now. Nikos and I. No, I want time to keep moving for a while, to give us the chance to get even closer and get married in New York. And then I want it to freeze. Time will be kind to me, at last, and keep us as we are; in love, forever."

Knowing how easy it was for Teri to work herself up, I didn't find her little outburst particularly surprising. It only takes someone to show her a little affection and she believes she's found the man of her dreams. I couldn't wholeheartedly share her joy. Not just because I'm suspicious of enthusiasm but also mainly because I'd seen her fall flat on her face so many times. Teri never learnt; she went on making the same mistakes, over and over. It would be annoying if it weren't so touching. She had the guts to challenge the world that rejected her every day on account of her transgender nature, and, at the same time, she was ready to forget all that she'd been through and give herself wholeheartedly to whoever took the trouble to give her some attention. While refusing to admit that some of those who courted her may have unsolved problems of their own. Of course, Nikos Zois seemed very different. He appeared happy about what was going on between them. He seemed sweetly, boyishly, in love with her.

"I'm even thinking of giving up work for him. Imagine that," she said.

I'd heard that before. Only major affairs prompted her to think of changing her profession. I was glad for her and wanted more than anything for things to go right, so that she wouldn't have to go on renting out her body, never mind her emotions. But I was a realist and didn't hold out much hope.

"Mr Zois seems to have done you some good."

"Just good? I'm radiant, man. Can't you see that? Radiant with joy, radiant at the sight of him, ra-di-ant, ra-di-ant."

Her voice was so gratingly off-key as she sang this that it almost made me laugh out loud. Teri had a fantastic voice, an ambisexual blending of the best elements of the male and female, and whenever she picked up a guitar and sang Hadjidakis, Loizos and Kaldaras' songs, people would stop whatever they were doing and sit spellbound. Even at school, where gangs of kids used to physically and psychologically torture her – if Drag, Maria and I didn't manage to get to them first – Teri's singing made everyone stop and listen. She bewitched them, even made them look human for a while. She could make some of her torturers change their behaviour towards her. I was a bit jealous. Of all the arts, only music has the power to awaken feelings where before there had only been darkness. Only music. Cinema could only record the darkness. Maria, Drag and I spent a whole decade, till we were in our mid-twenties, trying to persuade Teri to pursue a career in music, without success. She said she didn't want to commercialize it, she wanted to keep at least one part of her life pure and personal. We had no answer to that.

But now she was having fun. I let her finish mauling her made-up little song, her false long blond hair swaying this way and that, before trying to talk to her about her new love. Trying to bring her back down to earth and give her the softest landing I could.

"Was it him who asked you to give up work?"

"Of course not. It was my idea. I don't feel good when I go with this one and that, knowing that Nikos is thinking about me in bed with them. Doesn't feel right, eh?"

"So, *he* didn't say it was a problem."

"No, not at all. He took me in his arms – do you know how long it was since anyone had taken me in their arms? They're taking out their complexes on me, all those creeps, I often can't believe what I'm hearing – and by now I've heard it all. But *he*, he treats me so tenderly and hugs me and says that I can do what I want, he doesn't mind."

"He doesn't mind."

She nodded.

"Great. And he seems nice…"

"Adorable!"

"… but isn't that a bit strange?"

"What?"

"The closer he gets to you, the more he should object to sharing you."

"He's simply discreet. That's all. A gentleman."

"Right. And you discovered all these good points after a relationship of…"

"I know what you're going to say. That it takes time to get to know someone properly. But I do know him, deep down, our souls have connected since that first day at the centre, and we've been spending whole days together and I know that…"

"He's the one for you."

"Yes. He is."

She looked at me as if her relationship depended on the outcome of our conversation. I said nothing.

"What do you expect him to do? That's what I was doing when he met me. It's like in *Pretty Woman*: I'm Julia, he's Richard and, if at any time we fall out, you can be Barney Thompson, the hotel manager, to help us make up."

She had to explain who was who in the movie, because she'd put it on three times and each time I'd fallen asleep.

"From the little I recall, Richard wanted Julia's services exclusively."

Teri continued as if she'd never heard me.

"And since I'm Julia, *I* have to make the decision to change my life. Her relationship with Richard goes hand-in-hand with her personal development, see? 'Cause you're being a bit thick about this. What I'm trying to say is that whatever problems each of us has, as long as Nikos and I get along we have a chance of making it together, don't we? Everyone has a chance, even though most people fuck it up, but the chance exists, it's there, waiting for us. So why not? Why not go for it?"

Her phone rang. She picked up and I immediately knew that something was wrong.

"Got to go," she said, and ran to her bedroom to put on a sweater and change her shorts for a pair of jeans.

"What's up?" I asked.

"It was from the centre."

She was fighting back tears and indicated that she didn't want to talk about it.

"Please, please, come back tomorrow night," she said. "I really want to spend more time with you, especially now.

Nikos will be here too, I'll call him later. In the meantime, here's what you want."

She gave me a piece of paper out of her pocket on which was written "Lena Hnara", next to it a number. Aliki's friend.

"That's her phone number. Ring and arrange a meeting."

"I need her address, too. After everything that's happened she might be frightened and refuse to talk to me."

"I told you, she's a friend of mine and a good kid. There's no reason to go to her place; she'll talk."

"And if not?"

"I'll ring her right now, from the car, before you do. I'll tell her to expect your call. There's no way she won't come or say that she doesn't know anything. She owes me."

"Tell her I want to see her as soon as possible. Whatever time."

Teri nodded. She was all businesslike now, a different person altogether. She put her wallet and car keys in her jeans' back pocket. The handbag was the one female article she had never adopted.

"OK. OK. So, Nikos is fantastic, isn't he? Go now. Bye. Bye."

Walking to my car I remembered that Teri had called Hnara a "good kid". In *The Two Mrs Carrolls*, a '47 noir, in which Bogart played one of his most difficult roles, Barbara Stanwyck says: "Women are never wrong about women." Lena Hnara was willing to pay someone to kill her friend's husband. And the original Teri wasn't a pure-blooded woman.

I bore in mind the possibility that she was mistaken.

24

"It's Stratos. I'd like to see you," I told Vassilis Stathopoulos on the phone.

"I'd like to see you too," he replied.

His behaviour continued to baffle and surprise me. I couldn't say the same about his quick work to free Makis without any charges being laid against him. Makis had been released from custody almost immediately. I learnt that from Drag, who'd tried unsuccessfully to persuade Rizos to testify against him.

"That therapist wouldn't cooperate at all. He really seemed to take against me," Drag told me.

"He isn't crazy about cops," I told him.

"I'm not either!"

"If you tell him that, you might get a free session," I replied.

Vassilis suggested meeting in Piraeus, as he had something to do near the port. I mentioned an outdoor parking lot I knew well and he agreed to wait for me there alone, in three hours.

He was where he'd said he would be, and nobody was lurking around to hasten my demise. I knew because I'd arrived at our meeting point much earlier, to make sure I wouldn't encounter any ugly surprises. Every inch of the piers was filled with African refugees, women and their babies sleeping on the cement, covered with ragged coats, men begging for food at the shops around the port. The refugees had paid smugglers all they had to get them to Greece, in the hope that they would reach central and northern Europe. Now many were refusing to be sent back to Turkey. The government pamphlets stating that we loved them but they had to help us out strangely had little effect.

Reading the news on my mobile, I found out about the "something" Vassilis had to do. The largest Greek electronics company had got into financial trouble and was holding a press conference in its Piraeus headquarters to announce its bankruptcy. The workers' union had organized a protest and a counter press conference, together with their lawyer who was, of course, Vassilis, who had, of course, taken the case *pro bono*. If he carried on representing everyone who'd been sacked from corporations that were closing or relocating to the Balkans, he soon wouldn't be able to afford me.

Vassilis got in my car and I saw his eyes were all red. It wasn't emotion on seeing me, it was tear gas that the police had fired when the protest turned violent. A commentator on the radio was just saying that he thought Vassilis was a shoo-in to become an MP the next time there was an election, regardless of the scandal surrounding his wife's disappearance.

"The man's an idiot," said Vassilis.

I started the car, keeping an eye on the mirror to make sure we wouldn't be followed.

"So you don't intend to stand?" I asked him.

"I have my hands full with Aliki. And even if she got well and you sorted everything out, which party would I join?"

"I assume many of them would want you."

"But I hate all their guts."

Maybe he could form a party with Rizos, once he'd stopped sending goons to beat him up.

"If I behaved like they do, telling people they'll fight against austerity and then enforcing it, who'd believe me any more?"

"You're a lawyer; who believes you anyway?"

"I don't see it that way. I stand for different values."

Maybe he was an idealist. Or maybe not, if Aliki's accusations were true. Maybe the dirty money she said he earned was what would pay me.

"And if I told the truth about what needs to be done, who would want to listen?" he added.

"I have a few questions. Non-political ones," I told him, turning off the radio.

"About Makis, I'm sure. Why he took a shot at you at Rizos' office."

"That'd be a good place to start."

"I asked him to go and find Rizos. I'd told you I was going there myself, but I changed my mind. I don't think he'd tell me anything about Aliki that I might want to know."

"So you sent Makis, to beat the information out of him."

"If necessary. She's out there, all alone, lost and confused, and I still don't know who's after her. Behaving like a gentleman wouldn't do much good."

"How would killing me help you?"

"It wouldn't. That was Makis acting without authority. When he saw you with Aliki the night before last, he was convinced you'd taken up the contract on me."

"Aren't you afraid that I might have?"

"Stratos, I think you have your own principles. I think you really want to find out what's going on here, almost as much as I do. You want to find out before you decide what to do."

I didn't respond to that.

"If I wanted to kill you, what would I be doing at Rizos' office?"

"I know it doesn't make much sense, but it did to Makis. He was humiliated by the way you and Mr Dragas dealt with him the other day. And then he kept running into you… I apologize on his behalf. I have explicitly ordered him to stay away from you. It's in his interests as well."

"How come he appeared in Zografou the other night?"

"He has some contacts – an informer told him he'd seen Aliki there. Makis didn't trust him particularly; the guy is a drug addict so he didn't tell me. He's worked for me for years, you know, and he's very loyal. So he went to Zografou himself, to check it out, and there you were with Aliki. Are you going to tell me what she said, and if she's somewhere safe?"

His tone was almost pleading. He was no longer the totally in charge lawyer I'd watched at the live press conference an hour or so ago. He came on sincere, but I knew from Aliki what a control freak he was. And I never believed for a moment that he didn't really care about Aliki's former life.

"We didn't get much chance to talk. Makis interrupted us soon after I'd got there, and she thought I'd tipped him off – so now she's cut off all communication with me as well."

"Shit," he said.

I couldn't have said it better myself.

"I need to find her. I need to make sure she's safe, even if she doesn't want me to. And you need to discover who's after her. I'll pay for anything you need."

"If she doesn't want your help, you can't force her to come back."

"I can, until she's no longer in danger."

"And then what? You'll hold her against her will, until she stops hurting herself – which could take forever?"

"No. Once I know she's not in danger from others, she can do what she wants. I'll have done all I can for her. Maybe she'll appreciate it, but I wouldn't bet on it."

Each time we met I became less certain about the kind of guy he was and what he really wanted.

25

Maria called to ask me if it was a good time to come down-stairs – she immediately added that she had come across something that could be of interest to me and Drag. It was close to midnight, I was exhausted, I needed to get some sleep as soon as possible, and most of all I was upset by her comment. It meant that she wanted to make it very clear that nothing else could or would happen. I told her to come right down.

She arrived a couple of minutes later, wearing a blue shirt over her white nightgown. I had probably seen more beautiful sights in my life than her just standing casually in front of me, but I just couldn't remember them. What if I disregarded the unspoken rules between us? I wanted to believe she was fed up with Sotiris and ready to leave him. Maybe she just couldn't find the courage, and needed me to convince her this time it could work for us. Maybe deep down she wanted me to take her in my arms right there and then. Or maybe if I made a move I would cross the line and lose her for good.

"You look tired," she said.

"You look radiant," I replied.

"That's not fair."

"What isn't?"

"You can't respond to 'you look tired' with a compliment. Now you make me feel bad."

"Nothing to feel bad about. I'm intentionally looking tired. It's part of my new rugged look."

She smiled mischievously and I did nothing and the moment was gone.

"Do you know about Tor?" she asked me quickly, probably to make sure that it wouldn't return.

"Thor? The comic superhero?"

"Tor, the anonymity network."

I didn't know it. I knew there was something called the Deep Web, containing parts of the Internet that are not indexed by conventional search engines. I knew there was a subsection of it called the Dark Web, which many people in my profession frequented. I preferred to remain a Luddite.

"Yes, and it is thousands of times larger than the regular Internet. Tor software is the main way to connect," Maria said.

"The Dark Web has a bad reputation – what is a nice girl like you doing there?"

"I seem to be attracted to things and people with a bad reputation," she said and smiled again, that smile that still gave me sleepless nights. She quickly got back to business.

"There's a lot of inspiring stuff, for my work, there. Truly great artists who like to share and discuss their work only in these forums."

"Where they can meet with wonderful drug dealers, paedophiles and sex traffickers."

"And journalists trying to find hidden truths and activists working against dictatorships and wounded people looking for a place to rant."

I didn't reply. When she was feeling passionate about something, it was a good idea not to challenge her. Mainly because you'd lose.

"So, I was browsing around and thinking about you and Drag and Aliki and all that. I tried a new engine for deep searching through Tor's images. And I came across this."

She gave me the USB flash drive she was holding. I stuck it into my laptop and double clicked on the single file it contained. It was a photo with a text. The text read: "Look at the little whores, how they're all over each other. Fucking lezzies, I'd make you straight in one fuck."

You wouldn't call that the cultured web.

The women the text referred to did indeed look to be very close and their embrace, in the bar where they'd been photographed, seemed more than friendly. They were gazing at each other lovingly, not knowing that someone was taking their picture. They were both exquisitely beautiful – one of them naturally, the other thanks to plastic surgery. The two women in the picture were Aliki Stylianou and Elsa Dalla. Who "were polite to each other, nothing more", according to Peppas, the TV director and the other actors in their show.

The text included the hashtag "Stylianou" and the search engine Maria had used picked it up.

Another wrinkle to the case, if the photo was genuine. And there was something in it that made my spine tingle. Something that Maria couldn't have noticed, because she knew nothing about that story.

A couple of yards away from Aliki and Elsa, there was a really big guy having a drink and looking straight at the camera. He seemed to be enjoying himself immensely. Obviously he hadn't a clue that before long he'd be lying dead in an empty warehouse.

The man in the picture was Linesman.

26

My mobile rang again at 4.30 the next morning. Maybe it was a new custom I hadn't heard of.

"I've got news."

It was Drag, this time. I'd left him a message, and he decided to phone me at dawn. I had barely fallen asleep, after spending hours thinking about all those unanswered questions. Aliki, Vassilis, the role of Makis, Rizos and Elsa Dalla… I was pretty sure that there were connections that I was overlooking completely, missing links that I had to find out about. Maria's photo seemed to indicate a close relationship between Aliki and Elsa – or maybe it was just the two of them getting friendlier after a few drinks and being caught by someone taking pictures with their phone. "*I don't like to disappoint beautiful people. Why should I deny my body the pleasure?*" she had told me about women flirting with her. If Aliki and Elsa really had something going between them, this could explain Elsa driving Aliki's car, although that didn't explain who shot her and why. And what about Linesman? How could he have sneaked into the picture, so close to them? Was it planned, or just a coincidence? My head was buzzing, and I found myself remembering a walk with Maria years ago, when she was still with Drag. From Thissio Square towards Apostolou

Pavlou Street and then, through Eptahalkou, a narrow street with houses so low that you could jump up and touch their roofs. I remembered the expression on Maria's face and her guilty smile when I caught her looking at me with the same longing I had for her.

"News that can't wait?" I asked Drag.

"That kind, yes."

"Papi's?"

"In half an hour."

We couldn't meet at my place because of the risk of bumping into Maria. It's one of a long list of issues that are silently agreed between us. His only visit, back when he got excited by my new security system, had taken place when Maria was away for a couple of days.

I couldn't go to his place because it was infested with reporters wanting him to comment on the case. Drag's boss, without consulting him, had given a sketch artist my description, which had been passed to the media. It was indeed perfect, as Drag had told me. Not being a major suspect, I was only somewhere between pages three and five in the newspapers, and a short item on TV, but the publicity I was receiving was already more than enough.

"Aren't you going to at least tell me what it's about?" I asked Drag on the phone.

"Dalla. Before becoming Regoudis' girlfriend, she was having an affair with Vassilis Stathopoulos."

Whatever time I went to Papi's, Papi was always there. It was as though he never left the place.

"Maybe he never sleeps," Drag had suggested, when we'd first discussed it.

"You mean, *never?*"

"Yes, like Hawk."

I hadn't asked the obvious question because I didn't want to give him the pleasure. Drag loves to pepper his conversation with literary references as much as I love talking about film noir. I was sure that Hawk was the hero of some book Drag considered everyone should have read, and I knew he'd lecture me on it. So I said nothing, and after a few seconds of silence, Drag couldn't stand it.

"You do know who Hawk is?"

"Nope," I'd said.

"*You don't know Hawk?*"

"Only the bird."

"He's one of Robert B. Parker's most famous characters, Spenser's sidekick."

"Parker the mystery writer?"

That I knew from another conversation with Drag, which had begun: "*You don't know Robert B. Parker?*"

"'The mystery writer'? The *giant*, you mean," Drag said.

"Is he tall?"

Drag gave me a pitying look.

"'*The mystery writer*'. That's like calling Diego Armando Maradona '*a footballer*'."

Besides Parker, Drag is also a huge fan of Maradona.

"Tell me about Hawk."

Like most quick-tempered people, Drag quickly forgets his anger if you ask him to talk about something he loves.

"Hawk is the invincible muscle who's always there to help his friend Spenser when needed. He can be called at any time, is always ready, and always lethal."

"He must feel very tired."

"No, he just doesn't feel the need for sleep."

"Then he has a lot of free time to use his muscle."

"Exactly! Exactly!" Drag had shouted, so enthusiastically that a couple in their seventies, nearby, almost spilt their coffee.

"Drag…"

"*That's* Hawk!" he'd shouted again, with even greater fervour.

I knew that Drag would be in a good mood at half past five in the morning at Papi's. Not happy and smiling – the last time I'd seen him smile was when I'd taken him to Lake Beletsi. I had discovered it during one of my lonely walks at the foot of Parnitha, from the side of Afidnes and the housing estate of Ippokrates' Politeia, just a few hundred feet from a small church. The trees still standing on one side of the mountain, after the Parnitha's forest fire, were filling our lungs with oxygen, and the calm I felt around the water made me remember my adolescent dream to live on an island one day, in a hut by the sea. When two fawns appeared behind the bushes and stared at us in bewilderment, as we were ready in our underwear to dive, I saw a smile on Drag's face that I hadn't seen in years, probably since he and Maria were a couple. We spent hours by the lake, in silence, with the mild north-eastern wind caressing us. At some point, Drag wondered how it could be possible that this oasis, just twenty minutes off the National Road, was unknown to most Athenians. The obvious explanation is its distance from the city – when you spend a few hours commuting every day, the idea of driving another forty miles back and forth to find yourself close to nature isn't necessarily appealing. And you can't discover something beautiful if you don't know it exists.

So, Drag would be in a good mood, in the sense that he'd be fully alert and on the scent. The weather outside wasn't sharing my friend's good mood. Torrential rain lashing down. Angry. As if it wanted to scour the place clean. When rain-soaked, Athens seems vulnerable. Almost human.

Drag was already having a drink when I arrived. I was wearing a thick pair of glasses, hadn't shaved and was going to let my hair grow. I also had a stick in the car so that I could pretend to be lame, if necessary, since the description given by the waiter and doorman at La Luna both mentioned that I was an impressively well-built man.

Papi brought my drink without showing the slightest reaction to my appearance. A treasure.

"So?" I said.

"The less important stuff first. I spoke to three psychiatrists from the list that Vassilis gave us. All of them confirmed that Aliki had confessed that she cuts herself, that she hates him for loving her, that she wants to do him harm. And whatever he told us about the murder attempts is accurate: the Bulgarian motorcyclist, the spilt oil, everything. It seems our friend was telling the truth."

"On this occasion."

"On this occasion. Now for the good stuff. I spent hours with Regoudis, at his mansion in Ekali. Total kitsch. The PhD on the wall was the most tasteful thing there."

"I thought he kept that in his office."

"That's where his office is. He likes working at home, he told me, and to go around barefoot. He hates wearing shoes; they don't allow him to be in contact with the earth and feel its vibrations."

Total kitsch. I wasn't sure that I could trust Drag's aesthetic judgement, but I didn't raise the matter. Especially since he quickly passed on to a subject more interesting than Regoudis' bare feet.

"He's taken it personally; he's really set on finding the murderer. He told me that if it is a matter of money, however much, he'll pay."

Regoudis too was ready to splash money around… As if we were still living in that other Greece, when money seemed to grow on trees that everyone grabbed for. But a few hard facts would be more useful than money.

"The day before yesterday Regoudis couldn't see me because he was shattered by the murder – he had to be sedated. Not that he was much better yesterday. He asked Elsa's family to come to Athens for the funeral tomorrow, but they all declined. 'I'll be alone at her funeral,' he told me. 'She didn't even have any work friends. All alone. Almost as if she never existed.' He kept repeating it as he downed pills with whisky. I told him that if he kept on like that not even he would get to the funeral. Or he would be the guest of honour at the next one."

Drag, the perfect companion for a time of mourning.

"He said that's what he fears might happen, now he's lost her; that he'll be on his own like she was. He has a permanent staff of twelve in the villa – a Romanian and eleven Greeks – and he's asked them to come and talk to him to keep him company. The Romanian has been his right-hand man since their student days. Regoudis said that with such corruption everywhere the immigrants are the country's only hope, the only ones who are at all like the wonderful Greeks of the sixties."

"On pills and drink and yet he managed to do a social critique for you," I observed.

"When you have a PhD… The critique seemed to take his mind off his problems for a while."

Made sense. Someone who devotes a whole wall to his vanity wouldn't miss the chance to show how wise he is. He'll find time for pain later.

"Did he have anything more important to say?"

"He told me that he's put his own detectives on the case."

Journalists, detectives… Barnum and Bailey's Circus. The party was getting bigger and bigger.

We took a break as Papi brought us coffee and croissants. He'd gone to the jukebox and put on Louis Armstrong's *Keepin' Out of Mischief Now*. I exchanged looks with Papi who smiled and nodded. A treasure with a sense of humour.

I got out my mobile and showed Drag the snapshot of Aliki and Elsa. He seemed to enjoy the sexual implications, and said we'd have to look into that as well. But he had no more idea than I did about the truth of their relationship or the presence of Linesman right next to them.

"Maybe he'd just discovered photobombing," Drag said.

Then I told him that Maria had found the photo and the smile froze on his face. He recovered by telling me the reason he'd called me.

Elsa Dalla had come to Athens ten years ago, from her village, Rodia, just outside Grevena in north-western Greece. She wasn't particularly good-looking. She wasn't particularly smart. She didn't even have an artistic-sounding name – she was still using her real one, Evanthia Markantonopoulou. She also didn't have the foggiest idea about acting and had never in her life been to the theatre. But she did watch TV in the village: soap operas. She never missed an episode and knew them all by heart, foreign and Greek. And it seemed to her that what the actors were doing was easy. Being an actress would be so much better than becoming a nurse and wiping old people's bottoms, as her family were pressing her to do.

She failed her exams and took a night bus from the village to Athens. With little money in her pocket, she took a job in the first taverna she saw, to be able to pay the rent and eat for free. She had an affair with the taverna owner to get him to cover the drama school fees. Then she made the acquaintance of a handsome young actor who'd appeared in soap operas. She fell head over heels in love with him but kept up her affair with the taverna owner, as he was her financial support.

But the handsome young actor followed her one evening, discovered what she was up to and decided to go to the taverna and meet his rival face to face. Unfortunately for him, his rival wasn't the most principled person in the world. Sitting at the cash register with his stomach resting on the desk, the taverna owner listened carefully as the young actor cursed his mother, father and all the rest of his extended family, grabbed hold of his collar and threatened to beat the hell out of him if he didn't leave his girl alone. The taverna owner looked at Elsa, who didn't even dare breathe, and said: "Fine, friend. She's all yours." That statement had exactly the effect the taverna owner wanted: the actor relaxed for a couple of seconds, enough for the taverna owner to shift his stomach, open the drawer, take out a revolver, whisper: "No one insults my family" and send the young man to his grave. The funeral took place the next day, and that's where Vassilis Stathopoulos came in. The murdered actor, in spite of his love for the girl, was also having a relationship with a sixty-year-old who was a shareholder in one of the big TV channels – she was the one that had got him the soap opera part. After learning about the murder, she got straight on to Vassilis and asked him to make sure that the murderer was deported to one of those states in America that still has the death penalty. When Vassilis explained to her that it wasn't possible, because the crime had happened in Greece, she demanded he ensure that the murderer would grow old in solitary confinement, and never again see the light of day. Then she learnt that the cause for the murder wasn't just a drunken row, it was over a girl with whom her lover was involved. She phoned Vassilis again and insisted, with even more passion than before, that he get the taverna owner acquitted – she would cover all expenses.

Vassilis didn't manage to get the killer off completely, but as it was a crime of passion he only got eight years, which with good behaviour and a stay in an open prison was shortened to four. And Vassilis was bewitched by the girl he had cross-examined thoroughly, so much so that he asked her round for a meal at his place, just hours after the end of the trial. She obviously turned out to be even more bewitching, given that in the two years' relationship that followed, he showered her with gifts and paid for the plastic surgery that transformed her from an average-looking girl into the beautiful creature I had seen dead in Aliki's car. Never mind the few videos of her soap opera scenes on YouTube, which confirmed her impressive lack of any acting skills.

She wasn't bewitching enough for Vassilis to forgive her when he returned unexpectedly to the flat he had recently bought for her and found her riding a well-stacked young male model who had turned actor overnight and was now starring in another well-known soap opera.

"At least she stayed true to her soap operas," I said to Drag.

"Worshipped them and everyone starring in them. And she didn't hide it. Everything Regoudis told me about her previous relationships, he had found out from her. She was very open with him from the beginning, he said."

"Very open… I'm sure. And what he heard didn't bother him?…"

"Not at all. His Greek staff confirmed that – Regoudis was right; they weren't trustworthy, they came running to me to inform on him. He can't be the best of bosses. Only the Romanian guy didn't say anything at all. Anyway, they all agreed that once Regoudis had Elsa as his lover, he was confident she wouldn't go for anyone else. Why should she get mixed up with young actors when she had the producer between her thighs?"

"For the same reason that she got mixed up with young actors when she had Vassilis."

"No. For her it was all about getting into and staying in showbiz. Vassilis didn't have the connections to further her career. And he had banned her from posing naked to promote herself by showing off her newly acquired face and body. She actually believed he was holding her back, artistically."

"He doesn't like his women to show themselves off. He also stopped Aliki from modelling. Wasn't his previous relationship with Elsa widely known, though? Didn't they go around together?"

"No secret, according to Regoudis. Many references to them in the press, and a few photographs of them together, published again and again 'cause the magazines couldn't find any others. This agrees with the information I got that Vassilis was publicity-shy until he met and married Aliki."

"But since the relationship was known, the journalists will soon discover that one of Vassilis' former lovers has been found murdered in his wife's car."

"Relatively soon."

"Why 'relatively'?"

"It's not a new story. It's been almost eight years since our friend separated from Elsa. Even when they've found out her real name, it'll take a while before they connect her with the girl who once dated Vassilis. She had even more plastic surgery done after the separation. If you see photographs of her before and after, Elsa doesn't much resemble the girl she used to be."

Drag got out two photos and showed them to me. Elsa looked nothing like her old self. But she did resemble

Aliki. Regoudis, the producer, confirmed that Aliki was for Elsa an icon of perfect beauty and she really wanted to look like her. She had succeeded. She resembled her enough for the killers to be mistaken and murder her instead of Aliki. But how had she got in Aliki's car? And had the killers really made a mistake? Or could Elsa's murder have been another attempt to terrorize Aliki? Was it really coincidental that Elsa kept on with the plastic surgery to look like the new spouse of her ex?

"But they'll get there," Drag said. "Although she had officially changed her name, she put her parents' names on all her papers. You just have to phone them to get them effing and blinding at her. I know. I tried."

"And, somehow, this little detail that will become the talk of the town slipped Vassilis' memory both times he talked to us. Any ideas why?"

"None whatsoever. He also told us that he never had a relationship that lasted longer than a few months."

"Maybe for him twenty-four is a few."

"Maybe. Or maybe we should go and ask him a few more questions," Drag said.

"Are you sure? What about *Makis*?" I asked, putting on a show of fear.

Drag rarely smiles, and I really love it that I'm one of the few who can make him do so.

27

"Aren't we going to discuss how we're going to question him?" Drag asked as he parked outside Vassilis' house.

"Aren't we better without rehearsals?"

"Usually not."

"And you've just thought of it?" I said.

"You were on the phone all this time."

That was almost true. I was on the phone for most of the journey. I kept trying to get in touch with Aliki – sometimes her phone had no signal, making me hope that I would finally find her, but a few seconds later, the phone was switched off. Greek mobile operators. Service guaranteed. Drag could ask the public prosecutor to authorize the phone company to tell the police where Aliki was when she turned on her phone again. The first problem was that, with Greek bureaucracy, the whole process would take at least ten days. The second and more important problem was that, along with information on Aliki's location, the phone company would supply a list of calls to and from that particular phone over the last few months. Which meant that Teri's number would appear in the list, and we would have to persuade her to get rid of her SIM card to avoid getting traced and receiving a nice visit from the cops. Persuading her wasn't going to be easy. Her number was very popular in night-time Athens, where the needs of the flesh outweigh any financial crisis. Teri's yelling, if we told her to change it, would be heard from one end of the Attica Basin to the other. Drag and I agreed to let that rest for a few days in the hope of finding another way to locate Aliki.

During my unsuccessful attempts to phone Aliki I felt some kind of a bad premonition. I didn't know if it was about Aliki or us – Drag, Maria, Teri and me. My premonitions had never turned out true, something that only increased my anxiety that for the first time they would. I didn't have time to give it much thought, as a light suddenly dazzled Drag from behind. It wasn't a blaze of sunlight, as sullen clouds covered the city. We were in King Paul Avenue, behind the Asclepius Hospital, and for some time we had been ignoring the 70 mph speed limit and motoring around 120. Drag skidded to a halt, and the young policeman who'd been chasing us got out of his car wearing a blue raincoat two sizes too small for him. Slipping the safety off his gun, he shone his torch in Drag's face and asked to see his licence and insurance. Before Drag could even open his mouth the kid's cocky expression became one of awe.

"Oh! You are… you," he stammered.

At first Drag didn't know how to reply.

"Who else would I be?" he answered at last.

"You… you are… I saw you on television. You are the one who… has taken on the big case."

"I'm the one you flagged down."

"I didn't know, sir… I… that is… I'm sorry, I… carry on, please… sorry…"

The kid was still stuttering when Drag restarted the engine. I stuck my head out of the window to smell the sea. I couldn't see it, but I knew, I sensed that it was there – glad of the morning rain that was keeping it company. Everyone has their own idea about which of the senses is most important, the one they just couldn't live without. For me it's smell. You can learn to bear a lot of things. Seeing the concrete jungle of Athens stretch to the horizon and climb the burnt hills like some kind of poison ivy. Hearing horns sounding non-stop, accompanied by the constant swearing of drivers. Finding on your clothes, hands, face and hair the filth of the traffic. Watching the triple-parked Mercedes stay unmolested in the town centre while the police, across the street, are booking some poor worker on a Vespa for not wearing a helmet. But your sense of smell is there to safeguard you. To lift your feelings on those rare occasions when you get the chance to inhale the sea air or the scent of the person who loves you. Drag often reads the reviews to find out about good new detective novels. Riffling through a magazine one day he discovered that a famous Mexican writer, Guillermo Arriaga, lost his sense of smell at the age of thirteen on account of being punched repeatedly in the face. I don't know why, in general, people become authors, and from what they say when asked, they probably don't know themselves. But I think I know about Guillermo Arriaga, and I told Drag. That guy writes to smell the life around him.

"If his answers sound convincing, have you decided whether you'll accept Vassilis' proposal?" Drag said as we sat in the car outside Vassilis' house.

"I'll accept."

He didn't ask me why. Drag trusts me. It's enough for him to know my decision. If he *had* asked me, I couldn't have told him the precise reason, as I still wasn't sure who was telling the truth and who the lies. I would have had to find a way of explaining how a gorgeous, rich and successful woman seemed to me the weakest, unhappiest person I'd ever met, behind her faultless smile. Vassilis' proposal was attractive because it gave me a stake in the case involving his wife and a financial reason for accepting it, so that I wouldn't feel that I was violating my own professional rules. I had already filled in the amount on the lawyer's blank cheque. A hundred thousand euros. Without giving the name of the recipient. I would give him back the piece of paper just so he'd know what he would owe at the end. When Aliki's hunters had been rounded up. That was the real reason I'd accept: to take care of them, whoever they might be. And if one of them turned out to be Vassilis himself, I'd take care of him as well and take the money from Aliki, keeping his 30,000-euro deposit in return for deceiving me. But why should he deceive me? What did he have to gain? If he knew that I'd be after him, why not get Makis to off me when he had the chance? And if Vassilis was innocent, what was Aliki's mental state, how much help did she need? Now that she'd disappeared again, my best bet was to find the murderers of Elsa Dalla. Given that they had a tendency to turn anyone in their way into a sieve, 30,000 euros seemed like small consolation.

Drag got out of the Nissan and rang Vassilis' bell. The rain had died away to a gentle drizzle. Drag hitched up his appalling coat. A security camera flashed in his face and he waited patiently for whoever was behind the screen to look him over. It was, after all, only 6.50 a.m. – not the best time for making a visit. On the other hand, if your wife has disappeared and you fear for her life, it was as good a moment as any to allow someone in who was going to help find her. The wait lengthened. Drag and I exchanged glances. I knew what he was thinking. He wanted answers to his questions and he wanted them straight away. But if the gate didn't open he would have no option but to leave and return with a warrant. Our shared thoughts were interrupted by the most pleasant sound we could have heard. The security door trundled open and Drag leapt into the Nissan and drove furiously up the drive.

I was struck by the fact that the Rottweiler was nowhere to be seen or heard – whereas when we'd been there before it had let us know it was around. Nobody was waiting to greet us at the top of the wide marble steps that led to the front entrance – not even Makis. We got out of the car cautiously, in case the dog should appear, and went towards the steps. There, on the bottom step, we saw the first specks of blood. Not just one. Whoever had climbed those steps was bleeding heavily. At the top there was a big puddle of blood, in front of the door, which was open. I remembered that behind the door was a small hall, which led to the living room where we had spent that cosy evening with Vassilis and Makis. The hall was in darkness. The house was totally silent. It's incredible how much noise silence can make inside you, when it wants to. Even if you've lived through a hundred such silences, as Drag and I have, each time is like the first. Drag and I automatically, without saying anything, dropped down and crawled towards the door from opposite directions. In dangerous situations strength isn't in unity but in separateness. Split your team. Create many fronts. Confuse the enemy. We didn't know if we had an enemy and dangerous conditions to confront, but we needed to be ready. Drag aimed a kick at the door and it opened further. Still no sound from within.

"Stathopoulos!" Drag shouted.

"Shouldn't it be 'Stathopoule'?" I asked, being the better grammarian.

"You're a cretin," he murmured.

I'd been called worse.

"Police! Open up!" Drag shouted.

It seemed funny to me that he was shouting "police" with me next to him. It also seemed funny that he said "Open up!" when the door was already open. Not wanting to annoy him further, I kept quiet. Drag gestured that he was going in. He dived inside, not elegantly but effectively, as he got behind the nearest sofa without exposing himself as a target. He slowly raised his head, looked around, heard something and jumped up.

"Someone's getting out at the back!" he shouted, running through the house.

Drag never lets me know what move he's going to make next. He dives or runs like a maniac before I know what's going on. Our successes as a team owe more to our individual abilities and our willingness to look out for each other, than to our organizational skills.

I went into the living room ready for anything, but there was no one there. I ran to give Drag back-up, but by the time I'd reached the back door he was already turning around again, furious.

"I heard the car wheels skidding but by the time I got there it had gone – didn't even get a glimpse of it," he hissed.

"Vassilis?"

"Seems likely. But why wouldn't he want to see us?"

"Maybe he's worked out that we've found out about the things he forgot to tell us," I said, although I was pretty sure by now that Vassilis could offer a plausible explanation for anything.

"So what? You think he's worried I'm going to arrest him for concealing evidence? He could just not open the door. It just doesn't add up, Stratos."

"What does? Let's take a look at the blood outside."

"Yeah, it's…"

We had gone back to the living room when Drag broke off. I followed his look. We'd missed it when we ran through before. In the dark we hadn't noticed where the blood was leading. And though we'd both looked around, neither of us had looked up. Up high. The west end of the room ended in a glass window that went right up to the ceiling. You could stretch out on the sofa and gaze at the universe. A majestic sight, as long as there was nothing to disturb you. Such as Makis, hanging from the huge chandelier like a slaughtered animal, eyes wide open in terror.

28

Under the chandelier the blood had pooled in the shape of a crown, a huge circular stain encircled by many smaller ones. That's how it always is when blood falls from a height: you learn such things from hours in the field, and from talking to pathologists and forensic experts. Though my knowledge was not enough to explain why Makis' face and forehead were covered with symbols like hieroglyphs, written in lipstick.

Obviously, Makis was beyond help. But how the hell did he get up there? Who had managed to lift him and spike him on one of the big hooks sticking out of his back? And why go to so much trouble? It looked like a murder with a message, but what message did the hieroglyphs convey? The only link between everything that was going on was Vassilis himself, but he was incommunicado – Drag immediately tried calling him, but his mobile was turned off. If he wasn't around, who had opened the door to let us in, and why?

We found the Rottweiler covered in blood in a corner of the garden. Judging by the size of the wounds, it must have been blasted by a shotgun. Like Makis who, in addition to the hook in his back, had two gaping holes in his stomach. The rain started again. It lashed Drag's car as we drove to the Asclepius Piazza to find me a taxi before Drag returned to Vassilis' house and called his fellow cops... He told me he was hoping to find Vassilis and get some answers. I wasn't so optimistic. I saw a sick symmetry in the pattern of events: Aliki meets me to hire my services – Stathopoulos does the same; the macabre murder of Dalla in Aliki's car – the macabre murder of Makis in Vassilis' house; Aliki's mobile phone turned off – Stathopoulos' mobile phone turned off. Aliki's disappearance told me that Vassilis was going to disappear too. And with him my 100,000 euros fee. They'd both promised me money then broken off contact with me, one after the other. I had to find one of them, at least. I had to get a handle on this case, some facts that actually made sense. Not just for my sake, but also for Drag's – if my hunch was right and Vassilis had just disappeared, the pressure on Drag would be unbearable.

I had a few plans in mind.

29

She chose the place and time of our meeting. She was a lark, rather than an owl, she said, by way of explanation for fixing our rendezvous at eleven the next morning. Most of the larks I knew would be getting sleepy by eleven. We met in the top floor of the "Flocafé" in Stadiou Street, above Syntagma Square, an ideal place for such assignations: solitary enough for you not to be seen by the hordes of people who swarm in the streets all around and yet with enough customers to give you some cover. I was already drinking my espresso, reading a financial newspaper, which was warning yet again of the risk of the "sudden death" of the Greek economy if the government backed down on the new reforms that the Europeans demanded. I was wondering how this sudden death would affect my fees. Its slow painful death over the past few years hadn't affected me in the least, so I was about to conclude there would be no difference, when she arrived, twenty minutes late. Like Aliki. No doubt it was routine in their circle. I recognized her from a photo Teri had showed me. I stood up to attract her attention.

"Mr Gazis?"

"Mrs Hnara."

She gave me an up-and-down look. Her curiosity was natural: you don't meet a professional caretaker every day. I appraised her too. Although she wasn't a classical beauty, Lena Hnara immediately attracted your attention. Shoulder-length, raven-black hair, shining in the overcast light, mocking its dullness. A glow to her skin like that of a teenager, discreet touches of make-up, a confident step as she approached my table. The knee-length skirt and the turtleneck silk shirt she wore under her leather jacket hinted at a very fit body. It was only her face that lacked proportion – small eyes, round cheeks, a tiny nose with a bulge that made her nostrils look even tinier, a plump lower lip that almost eclipsed her upper one. As if she was the offspring of a bulky boxer and a tiny Chinese. She had the hair as well as the air of a model. Distant. Even when she ordered a green tea from the waiter it was as if there was an invisible wall between them. I remembered one of my old employers who had a thing about short, busty women. "Women are like houses," he told me. "The higher the ceiling the more impressive the house. But they don't keep the heat like the low-ceilinged ones." I had come across plenty of exceptions but Lena Hnara seemed to fit the rule. Every little detail about her told me immediately that she was alert to everything that was going on around her, but not part of it. Someone who wasn't cut off from the world but who was afraid of opening up to it, who kept themselves to themselves. I call them "observers". There are more and more of them. Lena Hnara looked like an observer who had been obliged to take an active part in her friend's life and suddenly found herself mixed up in a very strange case. Which disgusted her. *Involvement.* The worst, the most repugnant word for any observer. She glanced at the newspaper I had left open on the table. The headline was of course the disappearance of the Stathopoulos couple but I had already read the main article, which had absolutely no new information, and had gone on to the centre pages. Lena looked puzzled, as if it was inconceivable that I could have an interest in the stock exchange. She was right, I didn't. I had found the newspaper on the table and had just been riffling through as I waited for her.

"Well…" she said.

I waited.

"You must be the…"

Her tone was condescending.

"Yes," I said.

"Why did you insist on this meeting? What do you want?"

Abrupt. No manners. I missed Vassilis and his professional courtesy.

"Some answers."

"I already told you over the phone that I'm very concerned about the whole situation but I really don't know where Aliki is, and I want you to leave me alone. I don't like having dealings with people of your sort."

"Dealings like hiring me?"

"That was for Aliki."

"It's for her sake I wanted to talk. And here you are, regardless of your feelings."

"The only reason I'm here is that Teri is an old friend of mine and…"

"You owe her."

"I owe her, yes."

"I want you to answer some questions… To help me help Aliki."

"Out of pure altruism, I suppose."

I had begun to suspect she didn't particularly like me.

"Not at all. I took on her case. I want to finish the job, collect my fee and scram."

This wasn't true, at least not yet, but I had to present myself as an ally.

"How do I know that you're not mixed up in it? That you're not the one who kidnapped her? Your face is everywhere, you're the last one to have seen her."

"If I'd done her some injury, why would I want to talk to you?"

"To get more money, if you didn't manage to persuade Aliki to pay what you wanted. Maybe to threaten me…"

"Teri's your friend as well as mine. She wouldn't have set you up."

"Maybe you've fooled her as well."

She didn't know how close I was to Teri. She was off in some fantasy she didn't know how to get out of.

"Maybe you sold her some fairy tale that you want to help just to get me here to blackmail me because of my involvement…"

"Listen," I interrupted, "that's not what we're here for. You're in no danger from me. I'm just trying to find out what happened to your friend."

"Me too," she said, after a short pause. It seemed to me that she'd decided to be a little less defensive.

The waiter brought her tea, together with a big bowl full of different kinds of sugar and a jar of honey. Lena put all the sweet things on the next table, maybe to avoid temptation. She glanced at her watch.

"Go ahead. You've got exactly ten minutes."

"Very well, officer."

"I didn't come here for fun."

"I didn't come here to entertain you."

There was a rougher edge to my voice that startled her. She softened slightly.

"I have another appointment, in ten minutes…" she said, hesitantly.

"So you'll have to do some fast talking. Which will help us get to the truth and you to the next appointment. Do you know where your friend is?"

"No."

"There's been no communication between you at all after what happened with the car?"

"None. I keep trying to phone her but her mobile's switched off."

For a few seconds she was quiet. I just stared at her. Sometimes that works, sometimes it doesn't. This time it didn't. The only time anyone seemed genuine in this case was when they were describing how messed up the others were. Lena stared straight back at me, without blinking.

"Aliki told me, when we met, that you were going to lend her the money to pay me," I said.

"Yes."

"Because…?"

"I had it."

"Are you used to paying for such things?"

"Of course not."

"And you're not used to finding the right kind of person for this type of job?"

"No."

"It wasn't just a simple favour she asked you. Which means that you agreed with what she wanted to do."

"Yes."

"Usually, I'm the one who keeps his trap shut. But compared to you I'm a chatterbox."

She took a quick breath and burst out, "The guy's a bastard, understand? A real monster. A slime-bag."

"All the more reason to tell me the truth. It's your friend's husband you're talking about, right?"

We were surrounded by people, so I avoided mentioning names. Especially when the names were well known from the papers and TV.

"Correct. I told her I didn't like him right from the beginning."

"Strange. He's very popular."

"I know a lot of popular people. The reason they stay popular is that people don't know what they're really like. And him... he's the worst of all."

"What is it about him?"

"His eyes. Hazel eyes can be beautiful in women, but in men – they're like wolves. I've never met a decent man with hazel eyes. Sorry if..."

She opened her palms and gestured towards me. She wasn't really sorry – I was perfect proof of her theory.

"No offence taken," I said.

"His eyes aren't quite like yours, but... I can't describe them... Have you ever seen him close up?"

"Yes."

"When he looks at you, he's half-angel and half-devil. That's the best way I can describe it. The *only* way."

"But you can't judge him just by his eyes."

"He treated her really badly. Abusively. When we were with our friends, Aliki's and mine, without his acquaintances around – I don't say 'friends' because he doesn't have any – he was polite and didn't care if Aliki showed her ignorance or talked nonsense. He would laugh and seem at ease, caring, he'd take her in his arms and explain what she'd got wrong. That was the angelic look, the one that made you think that Aliki was the luckiest woman in the world to have found him. But, if one of his acquaintances was there, oh, he was *scary*. Many times I've been there when he put her down because he didn't like what she was saying, treating her like some worthless bimbo, not his wife. He could be so sarcastic that people just stared at him, their smiles frozen, not knowing how to hide their embarrassment. One evening I was at their house and Aliki said something – I don't remember what – to a theatre director, one of those artistic snobs who puts on plays for an audience of five. I think that Aliki had been to one of her productions and was politely telling her what she thought when Vassilis turned, in front of everybody, and said loudly, 'What do you expect from a model who thinks she's an actress?… Aliki, my dear, I've told you a thousand times your views are like cosmetic surgery: best kept to yourself.'"

"At least he said 'my dear'."

"She ran upstairs and I followed to comfort her. She cried for an hour and didn't come down again, but when I told her yet again that she should come and stay with me, she wouldn't listen. That same evening the bastard beat her up, just for leaving him alone with the guests."

"Did you actually witness one of those beatings, or any other act of violence?"

"Of course not. He kept that private."

"So, you only know about the beating from Aliki. And you believe her because of the way he generally treated her."

"It doesn't matter what I believe. Aliki had so many scars that... I suppose you spoke to him or one of his lackeys and they told you that nonsense he gives to the psychiatrists; that she did it all to herself."

"He's not the only one who said so. She confirmed it too."

"Where? To whom? To *his* psychiatrist friends? What else could she say? She was scared that if she told the truth they would all gang up against her, have her certified insane and shut up in some madhouse. To avoid that she'd confess to anything. But she told the truth to her *own* therapist. That's what she needed – a psychologist, not a psychiatrist. For a long time I listened, but in the end I persuaded her to go and see someone qualified whom she could trust."

"Antonis Rizos."

"Yes."

She paused for a second, a bit surprised. Maybe I wasn't just a dumb hired gun, after all.

"He's my psychologist as well. Antonis and I are the only people Aliki confides in. At the start we went to him together, several times. It was his suggestion, to help her open up. At first she was a bit wary of confessing to a stranger but when he earned her trust he helped her a lot, restoring some of her confidence, despite what was happening at home."

"Did you ever advise her – you or Dr Rizos – to get a divorce?"

"Antonis, never. A therapist can't suggest anything like that without first speaking to the patient's partner, and that was naturally out of the question because if Vassilis found out that Aliki had told the actual truth… there's no telling what would happen."

"And you?"

"I tried. I tried my best to get her to split from him. She was too scared. She knows how powerful and ruthless he is. Aliki has no one to turn to, except me. Of course, I told her that my husband and I would protect her. But in our circle everybody knows each other – Vassilis has even appeared in court on behalf of my husband. That was some time ago, and he lost the case, by the way. Though the media have created this image of him as the lawyer who never loses. Anyway, Aliki doesn't believe it's possible for anyone to really protect her or that anyone would put themselves out for her. Only me, and she didn't want to put me in danger, because she knew that his threats were no joke; the guy's a psycho."

"Doesn't hiring me put you in danger? What will happen if things go wrong and he finds out?"

"You're supposed to be very good at your job. So it wouldn't come to that."

"Thanks for the vote of confidence."

I offered her a cigarette.

"Disgusting habit," she said, and looked around in annoyance to see more than half of the customers smoking. Laws in Greece are only written to be broken.

I lit my own cigarette and prepared to continue the questioning, but she got in first.

"So you've actually met him?" she asked.

"Yes."

"And… why…?"

"Why didn't I do the job…? Nobody's paid me anything yet."

Actually, I had received Vassilis' down payment, but I kept that information to myself.

"Does he know?"

"He knows that Aliki approached me to do the job. He didn't say anything about you, though."

She shivered suddenly. It might have been the air conditioning. Or it might have been that Vassilis terrified her.

"And where is he now?" she asked.

"He doesn't tell me his movements."

"Because they say on the news he's disappeared... do you think he's alright?"

"Obviously you hope he's not. What are you not telling me?"

"I don't know what you mean."

"Maybe you and Aliki have approached someone else to do the job. To be doubly sure."

"Hiring you was a big enough involvement for me."

And involvement was something she usually avoided.

She rubbed her eyes, took a deep breath. I drank the last swallows of the espresso to give her time to pull herself together. She didn't succeed. She was close to tears.

"This can't be happening to me. I'm a... normal person. This isn't... isn't... this happens to criminals in the movies, not... I never imagined my life... like this."

As if anyone ever imagined their life as it turned out to be. I let her take a few more deep breaths, which seemed to do her good, because she came back with a question.

"What do you think has happened?" she asked. "How can they both disappear?"

"I told you, that's what I'm trying to find out. I don't have any theories. Logic tells me that either one of them

has polished off the other and is hiding, or that someone else has harmed both of them. Unless they're both
involved in something and hiding away together. And of
course there is just the possibility that their relationship
improved so much that they walked off into the sunset."

"But what about the murder of the bodyguard? I read
about it… I mean, how could Aliki ever do something like
that? She hasn't got it in her, she could never…"

Hang him on the chandelier, she meant, but couldn't say
it. She didn't want to put words to the image she'd only
read about.

"That's why I asked you whether you had hired anyone
else."

"No, no… That is, I can't say for certain, but I do know
Aliki. No chance… She's so good-hearted, even when we
talked about getting someone… *you,* that is… it was such
a struggle for her, we'd been discussing it for months.
It was only after the second attempt on her life that she
started to realize that there was no other way, and when
she saw that his behaviour was getting steadily worse she
finally decided. But if you are right and one of them has
killed the other… and since Aliki can't be the one who
killed the bodyguard…"

She bent her head, pinched the bridge of her nose
and closed her eyes. She didn't want to follow that train
of thought any further. To tell the truth, neither did I.

"Tell me about the murder attempts," I said.

Her account was the same as Aliki's. Almost.

"You should have seen him when he was jealous… One
night Aliki and I got back late. We'd been to the theatre
and he knew that she was with me but instead of going

straight home we stopped off for a drink, to catch up on each other's news. Knowing how he could be, she'd phoned to let him know but couldn't get through to him and then he kept calling her but her battery was flat. As we were standing on their doorstep saying goodbye he threw open the door, grabbed her by the arm, pulled her in and slammed the door in my face. He thought that I was helping her have an affair, Aliki told me when I next saw her, a week later – he beat her up and kept her in the house for days."

Parallel universes. The phrase was spinning around in my brain all the time I was listening to her. I'd seen it on the back cover of a detective novel Drag was reading. I don't know what it was about, but that phrase stuck with me: "Parallel universes". Aliki and Lena, on the one hand, and Vassilis on the other. At the beginning I had thought that someone – maybe more than one – was telling lies. Now, though, it seemed as if they were living in different worlds in which they associated with the same people, but behaved totally differently in each one.

"When I talked to Vassilis he admitted that at the beginning, he'd often been really jealous. But he said that once he saw the problems Aliki had had, he got over it," I told her.

"She didn't have any problems before she met him. *He* was her problem. Before she married, Aliki was the happiest kid in the world. Literally, a kid. She really enjoyed life and playing around."

"Playing around with people?"

"Meaning?"

"She told me it didn't matter to her whether someone she was attracted to was a guy or a girl."

Her mouth snapped shut again.

"What are you getting at?" she asked.

Until she asked, I wasn't getting at anything. I was just fishing for information. But after her question, I had something to get at.

"First of all, I wanted to see if the idea of her having a girlfriend shocked you. I see it didn't."

"So?"

"So, I'll lay it on the line."

"Lay what on the line?"

"You're not stupid."

"Big compliment – from a murderer."

I don't like that word. "Caretaker," I corrected.

Her reply came in the form of a sarcastic look. I stared back at her. "And the difference between the two is...?" she asked, contemptuously.

"A caretaker takes a job to correct something that's wrong. Someone who carries out the other sort of job you mentioned just sees bodies in front of him. And you didn't answer my question."

"I'm not obliged to answer anything."

"That's right. You're not."

For the next minute the silence between us was noisier than all the other tables put together. It was Lena who put an end to it.

"Aliki and I are best friends. Just that. Nothing else. I do know about her preferences, yes – or rather, her lack of them. She likes beautiful people, without distinction. Once, when we'd first met – we were about eighteen – we were at a party together and we found ourselves alone in the kitchen. We'd had a bit to drink – she kissed me. I was so surprised I just stood there with my mouth open so she kissed me again. 'To shut your mouth,' she said. I still had no idea what to say, but I didn't realize how surprised I really was. Are you ever truly unaware when someone's about to kiss you? I don't think so."

"Did you like it?"

"The kiss? I'd be lying, if I said I didn't. But that's as far as it went. I liked it, but I didn't want to go any further. And even if I did it would be against my conservative upbringing. But I didn't. I've never felt any real attraction towards another woman. For Aliki either. So we just dropped the subject. I think that's why we are so close, why she tells me everything. Maybe I'm the only person who doesn't want to sleep with her. So she knows that I'm sincere in everything I say to her."

I noticed that she constantly spoke of her friend in the present tense. The possibility that Aliki was dead must have occurred to her, but she wasn't accepting it. This could either mean she knew very little about her friend's disappearance, or that she knew quite a lot, but was clever enough to hide it.

"You asked me whether she played with people before she met *him*. Yes, she did, without being aware of what she was doing. I often told her that behaving like a kid might be fun for a while for whoever she was with, but when she dropped them they were destroyed. When Aliki was with someone she was *lost*. If we all went out together I often didn't recognize her, she wasn't the Aliki I knew. She somehow became whatever her new date wanted her to be. A chameleon. When I asked her about it she said that she just wanted to make them happy, that love was about giving, and she got a kick out of fulfilling someone else's dream. It was also good for her, she said, because it allowed her to act and she had always dreamt of becoming an actress. I told her that behaving like that would prevent anyone from falling in love with her for what she really was, but she wasn't convinced. 'Even if they fell for what I was,' she said, 'how long would it last? Whereas if I'm their dream, they'll put me on a pedestal and adore me forever.'"

"Maybe one of those adoring people couldn't stand losing her."

"You mean one of them could be behind all this…? No way. All her exes worship her. Even today. She keeps in touch with them all and no one's ever said a mean word against her. I've never understood how she does it – dumps them and still has them at her feet, thankful that she was just walking out, not completely disappearing from their lives."

"You sound almost jealous."

"Not 'almost'. I *am* jealous. I've never seen such charisma in anybody else. Aliki *captures* everyone around her."

I had an inkling of what she was talking about.

"I asked her once how it was possible not to have had a fight with at least one of her exes; there must surely have been one unhappy guy who was truly maddened by their separation. I thought I knew a thing or two about the psychology of people in love but she looked at me, surprised, as if I was telling her something that had never crossed her mind, as if I were an alien speaking a language she didn't understand. 'Sex is a feast,' she said. 'How can someone hold a grudge against someone else if they've feasted so deliciously together?' The mad guy turned out to be the one she married – and he'll do anything to keep her."

I thought it was time to shock her with a surprise question. "What do you know about Vassilis and Elsa Dalla?"

"I know they were lovers, once, for a while."

Her answer came so quickly I was convinced it was genuine. "Aliki told me," she continued. "*He* liked to boast about his former exploits. Not in public – he'd never soil his name, but in private, with the boys, you know the kind of thing. I've heard about it from my husband who can't stand them – the detailed way they describe their lovers: what they're like in bed, what they're like naked, what shape this has or that... And *he* was always the one who went into most detail. A slime-bag – I told you so right from the beginning. Aliki didn't want to know anything about his earlier love life but he sat down and laid it all out in front of her, whether she liked it or not. Then he demanded that she tell him everything about herself in return. Luckily, though, it was one of the few things he didn't manage to make her do. God help us if he had – the list is so long it would have plunged him into even deeper obsession. If that's possible."

I remembered Vassilis talking about the same subject, at his house.

She saw things differently. She insisted I had to be open about my past and write down the names of all my former lovers. I continued to believe in the power of ignorance, and learnt nothing at all about hers.

So many different versions of the truth. Almost a joke. Good liars spice their lies with truth to make them more convincing. We were dealing with some pretty bad liars.

"And how did Aliki feel about working with one of his former lovers?"

"They didn't exactly work together. They worked in the same studio, but it was rare for them to appear together in a scene. It bothered her. Crazy as it sounds, it did. She felt uncomfortable with Elsa. She'd give her just a formal greeting and leave."

Just a formal greeting. Yes, I'd seen evidence of the formality between Aliki and Elsa in that bar photo.

"I often asked her why she minded. It would be great if Vassilis still wanted Elsa and she him, which was probably the case, judging from all the plastic surgery she'd done to look like Aliki. Let them go on to live in bliss together for the next 200 years, if only he would leave Aliki alone. Why did she mind? Even she couldn't explain it: 'How do I know? He's my husband. He's still my husband, whatever he's done, and from the way he behaves he shows me that he wants me,' she said. That's the key, for her – to feel wanted by everybody. Just a kid, you see. A kid. With no idea what she's doing. And it was great when she finally got over herself and decided that she definitely didn't want to be with him any longer."

"During our talk, Aliki mentioned his behaviour towards her after the incident with the video."

"What video?"

"The one with the banker."

"I don't know what you're talking about."

"Aliki never mentioned the relationship she had with a big-shot banker?"

She thought a while.

"No. Banker... no. I'm trying to think back if there might have been... but no. Unless... unless it was one of those one-night stands, one of those she was ashamed to tell me about… But a relationship… no. I would know about it."

One-night stands. I remembered Aliki telling me that she had slept with two or three people on the same day. But I remembered even better her telling me that she had a *relationship* with the banker on the video. So she did keep secrets from her best friend. Of course, if she didn't tell Lena about her spur-of-the-moment lays, she had no reason to confess them to me; but there was also no reason why she should hide them from me, which is why she spoke so openly at La Luna. Plus, how easy would it have been to have a threesome with the banker and her fan, with the camera recording everything, if it was just a one-night stand? Such situations demand trust in the other two sexual partners. Or perhaps I was overanalysing. From the complete picture of Aliki Stylianou that I was starting to form, maybe everything *was* that simple for her, maybe sex simply didn't cause her any worries. There are those who indulge themselves whenever the fancy takes them; maybe Elsa was also one of them. Parallel lives: Aliki and Elsa both came from the provinces; both were dazzled by the stage; both had had relationships with powerful men; they shared at least one lover. Maybe more, if the allegation that Athens is one huge bed is true – I've never put it to the test. Maybe Elsa and Aliki were lovers, but only one of them had been blessed with unbelievable natural beauty, while the other had sought the creative attentions of the plastic surgeon. The two looked so alike that one might have died in the place of the other, but the opposite could well have happened.

"Just one more question," I told Lena.

She glanced at her watch.

"It's been a whole hour!" she exclaimed.

"See, when you're in the right company…"

She tried to reassume her distant manner but quickly abandoned the attempt.

"I didn't really have an appointment."

"I guessed. Aliki had a steady relationship before her marriage – I suppose you know that."

"Yes."

"When and who with?"

"For eight, maybe nine months, just before she got to know Vassilis. Very ironic, that."

"What?"

"That she found herself working with her old lover after three years."

"Working where?"

"Her old lover, the steady one, was Hermes Peppas. The director of the series she was acting in, with Dalla."

The one who'd assured Drag that Aliki and Elsa never went around together.

"But they separated on very amicable terms. Hermes would never hurt her. They spent those few months together and then, though they wanted only the best for each other, they saw that as a relationship it just wasn't working – he is very eccentric in his personal life. And when they met again during filming, Aliki told me that he behaved impeccably. Like close friends."

I tried to get my thoughts into some kind of order, but something told me that I still didn't know the half of it. The relationships were hopelessly tangled and I still didn't have a firm lead to follow.

"Is that it, then?" Lena asked, taking out her purse to pay the bill.

I gestured to her to put it back in her bag, "That's it. Thanks."

She got up and put on her coat. It may have had a designer label, but I've never paid enough attention to distinguish one from another. "Will you tell me if you come up with any leads or will I have to watch it on the news?"

"I'll tell you."

"Promise?"

She smiled.

"I promise."

"This hour, talking here with you, was the strangest of my life," she said as she was leaving.

"I'll take that as a compliment," I told her.

I wasn't sure she'd told me all she knew, but it was a good start. I didn't let on about how this case had affected me, either. For example, I didn't tell her that I had started to sleep very little. I didn't tell her that in the little sleep I got the night before, I'd dreamt of Aliki shouting for help. And I didn't tell Lena, when we said goodbye, that even if what Aliki had told me was only a figment of her troubled mind, I really, really wanted to help her.

30

Teri seemed to have aged a decade since I last saw her, when I visited her that evening.

"Tell me," I said.

She didn't reply immediately. When Teri doesn't talk, things aren't good. When she's expecting to meet her new love in a couple of hours and isn't anxious about her new manicure, her highlights and extensions, and whether she looks like a goddess or merely an empress, things are even worse.

"Six months ago, we got a call at the centre," she said finally. She seemed to be on the verge of tears, but she wouldn't let herself cry. "The call was from a six-year-old boy, Fanis. His mum was divorced, raising Fanis and his brother by herself. She'd been laid off from one of the big companies that fled the country and relocated to Bulgaria to escape the taxation. She started doing drugs before she was fired, and didn't have the money to pay afterwards. She ended up living with her dealer, working as a hooker. The dealer hit the kids, more and more each day. They got on his nerves just for being around. Fanis' brother was two and Fanis often got in the way to save him, took the beatings for him. One day he wasn't quick enough. The baby was taken to the hospital, and barely survived. Their mum said the baby had fallen; it was an accident. Fanis called us to say it wasn't. We called the police, persuaded the mother to go to rehab, took the kids with us to the centre. I spent weeks with the boys. The baby stopped having seizures from his brain injuries. Their mum got out of rehab and took them back two days ago, for a trial period. Today she killed Fanis, while he was sleeping. Stabbed him to death, for ruining her life."

I thought she might collapse. I moved to hug her. She hit my arms, kicked me.

"No!" she shouted. She was as strong as an ox, but I was stronger. After a while, she stopped kicking.

"We've got the baby. The baby is safe. Fanis would have been happy with that," she said.

For me, silence is the best medicine. For Teri, it was talking. I asked just enough questions to let her dump it all on me, telling me about the horrors she went through every day. You might have thought that being plunged into poverty would have brought you closer to your kids. But maybe it was the suddenness of the plunge that was the problem.

"I think you should focus on killing child abusers," she said. "I'm sure I could find the money to pay you. You're already my hero for ridding the world of villains. Why not go further, and get rid of the worst of the worst?"

After a while, she got up and brought me her special treat. She hadn't made it for me – she wanted to impress Nikos – but I wasn't complaining. Her speciality is a chocolate dessert made with biscuits. It sounds simple. It isn't. It is the food of the gods – her own recipe, which she doesn't give to anybody, however much they beg her for it. It takes her days to get the ingredients together because she has to order them from sources she won't reveal. But once she's made it, however self-controlled you are, you simply can't stop wolfing it down till you've polished off the plate. Her lamb espetadas have nothing on this cake, and Drag is its greatest fan. He is always the first to sit at the table, glaring angrily at anyone who dares take a second portion. Once we attacked the cake so greedily that there was none left for Teri. Wanting to sample her own cooking, she reached out to take a mouthful from Drag's plate. He stabbed her hand with his fork and carried on eating while Teri danced around swearing at the pain and smiling because her cake was a hit yet again.

This time, Drag was with us though he didn't know it, as we were eating the cake in front of Teri's huge plasma TV. He seemed to be even more pissed off than the last time we were all together, when she stripped to the waist and danced in front of him. Now he had to face dozens of journalists waiting to interview him in a press conference broadcast live by all the major TV stations. It was timed to go out on the main news bulletins, and however much Drag hated publicity he couldn't wriggle out of it this time. He was fast becoming a member of every Greek family who watched the eight o'clock news. He didn't stand much chance of working undercover in the near future.

"Let's see if Mr Dragas will be more forthcoming than he was this morning," the newscaster said. They had shown edited footage from Drag's morning visit to the chief of police, when he was ambushed by a score of reporters. He'd tried to brush them aside but they clung to him like flies on a horse.

"Do you have any clues as to the whereabouts of Vassilis Stathopoulos?"

"We are investigating."

"Can you say whether he is safe, or whether he might be the victim of a criminal act?"

"We're investigating that as well."

"What do you have to tell us about Aliki Stylianou?"

"Nothing."

And then he dodged to one side, jumped over the TV cables, pushed a reporter out of the way, and made his escape.

"But how can he walk around in that thing? Doesn't anybody ever wash or iron it?" Teri exclaimed. It did look as if Drag slept in his raincoat.

"One more unprecedented display of Mr Dragas' disregard for the media," a commentator said. *One more unprecedented display.* One more tribute to the Greek educational system that these TV commentators were so articulate.

But this evening Drag couldn't get away by jumping over cables. The journalists weren't going to let him. Their TV stations and newspapers needed news and they needed it right away. The endless interviews with lawyers, actors and models who had at some point worked with Vassilis, Aliki and Elsa Dalla were OK to fill airtime, but Drag was the real deal.

"Mr Dragas, every day we've been asking questions of burning interest to our audience, and it seems as though nobody has anything to say. Can you give us some meaningful answers? Can you give us *any* answers?" a particularly ugly reporter exploded. Seeing that Drag wasn't in a hurry to respond, he tried again: "Because the obvious question is…" he paused dramatically. "The obvious question is how is it possible that a well-known actress could have been murdered in the car of a famous model and then for the model and her husband, one of the most prominent men in Greece, to simply disappear? Do you suspect that they have been kidnapped or murdered? How is it that the police have come up with absolutely no clues, and have absolutely nothing to say by way of explanation?"

"That's three questions," Drag said.

Teri punched the air and shouted "Give it to them, Rocky!"

"Are you here to make jokes, Mr Dragas, or are you going to respond? How-is-that-possible?"

"What you describe is what happened," Drag answered.

"Mr Dragas, could you confirm that you requested permission from the chief of police to conduct all the questioning yourself, because you don't trust your fellow officers?" That was asked by a reporter from one of the tabloids who had offered Drag 20,000 euros to leak findings from the investigation, to which Drag had responded by spitting on his shoes. "So you want more?" the reporter had asked.

"Mr Dragas, is it true that you have trouble dealing with your subordinates? That's what our information suggests and, if it's correct, how can this case possibly proceed?" asked another journalist, getting in on the act.

Drag never had problems dealing with his subordinates. It is with his superiors that he often has problems. They were the ones leaking stuff about him to the press.

"Mr Dragas, we have information that links the case to drug-smuggling rings. Have you any comment?"

"Mr Dragas, do you suspect that the disappearances are linked to the recent revelations of corruption in the judicial system?"

"Mr Dragas, have you discovered what the symbols found on the body of Makis Zyridis mean?"

"We're investigating," Drag answered.

Drag had told me that the symbols had not led anywhere. They had been faxed to the Egyptian Embassy and when the specialists there threw up their hands, the fax was forwarded to the archaeological service in Cairo. There, they found someone who explained that there are around 5,000 known hieroglyphic characters, and most of the symbols inscribed on Makis' body bore no resemblance to any of them. But the archaeologist happened also to have made a study of Mayan hieroglyphics and he believed that they could be from that culture. The problem was that when he deciphered them they apparently meant "good mountain baby now".

"Mr Dragas, could you confirm whether or not Aliki Stylianou belongs to an extremist religious group?"

"Mr Dragas, really, do you have the slightest bit of information to give us about this case or are we completely wasting our time here?"

You could hardly have fed Drag a better exit line.

"I'd say you are wasting your time. Thanks very much," he said, getting up and disappearing through the door behind him. The press conference had finished in fifteen minutes, instead of the scheduled hour. Drag's bosses would be foaming at the mouth as they watched the reporters rush to their cameras to lambast the police in general and Drag in particular.

"Do you know what you and Drag remind me of?" Teri said.

"No, but I'm about to find out."

"A line from Kubrick's *The Killing*."

I'd been more successful in influencing Teri's taste in movies than her attempts to make me like *Pretty Woman*.

"All these years we've been friends and we remind you of *one* line?" I told her.

"It's the only one that fits you two like a glove. Actually, the film would have been much more interesting if Kubrick had gone further in exploring that theme…"

"Which line and what theme?"

"The relation between a cop and a criminal. The hero of the film was Sterling Hayden. In 1941 Paramount advertised him as the handsomest actor in the world, did you know that?"

"No."

"Yes, and in other adverts they called him 'The beautiful, blond, Viking god'."

"Is this information really essential?"

"No, but it's great! Unfortunately, he was completely heterosexual, the dope – not the slightest hint that he might have been one of us. He married the same woman three times, can you believe it? And separated three times. How long does it take for him to get the message?"

"Are you going to tell me the line?" I cut her off.

"Yes… so… Sterling Hayden plays Johnny Clay, a thief who has been freed after spending five years in Alcatraz, and is planning to pull off a big one and steal two million dollars from a racetrack."

"I know the story. It's the line I want."

"I'm *getting* there, Mr Patience. So, Clay is talking to Joe Piano, the manager of a motel, and says: 'This afternoon a friend of mine is stopping by and leaving a bundle for me. He's a cop.' 'A cop?' asks the other. 'Yeah, yeah he drives a prowl car.' 'Funny kind of a friend to have,' Joe tells him. And Clay answers: 'He's a funny kind of cop.' The whole film should have been about the relationship between Clay and the cop, or you and Drag, except you'll never go to prison, but Kubrick blew it."

I remembered the film vaguely, though not that particular line.

"Speaking of directors, have you heard of Hermes Peppas, who directed Aliki's TV series?"

Teri gave me a look. Maybe I should have heard of him? Drag hadn't either; he'd referred to him as "a certain Peppas".

"You really don't know him, or you're pulling my leg?"

"I really don't. And neither does Drag," I quickly added.

"Ah, Drag, who has his finger on the cultural pulse of Greece," Teri said.

She had a point there. Drag didn't know any celebrities, but at least he knew about Robert B. Parker and Maradona.

"You two must be the only Greeks who don't know the guy."

"And everybody else knows him because…"

"OK. Film gossip for dummies."

I nodded.

According to Teri, Hermes Peppas, forty-five, was one of the biggest stars in Greek show business because he'd done fabulously well in America before his career took a nosedive. He had been a child wonder. While still a twenty-year-old student he made two shorts, which won prizes at big international festivals. Then he worked for a year as assistant to a director of low-budget horror films, partly for the experience and partly for the half-naked beauties in torn clothes who always appeared in such films and screamed shortly before being slaughtered by a psychotic murderer. Having achieved his main aim, which was to rip off in private as many of these dresses as he could get his hands on, Peppas managed to persuade a producer to trust him as first director of a new horror film.

The film's main attraction was that it would be terrifying while made on a shoestring, thanks to Peppas' screenplay, which he read out loud to the producer – the producer considered reading a waste of time. Peppas' screenplay was itself a rip-off. He had taken a third-rate horror film from the seventies, and just changed the names. The producer agreed, with the proviso that Peppas would regularly inform a member of the production company how the film was going. This member was a woman who fell madly in love with the young director. On the first day of shooting, Peppas told the actors that certain changes were to be made in the script, dumped it in the bin and took out the copies of his real screenplay. He had written a spoof of the horror genre, mocking every stereotype and keeping to tradition only inasmuch as it included the torn dresses of the shrieking lovelies. The film did so well at the box office that the producer forgave Peppas for taking him in.

His second film did even better, and was a real smash. Having hit his stride, Peppas wrote and directed two films within six months, which were among the top box office hits of that year. But the critics loathed the infantile comedies and horror spoofs he was making. "Do they improve people?" a journalist asked him once. "I'm not interested in improving anyone," growled Peppas, "I just want people to have a good time." His target group, aged between fifteen and twenty-two, concurred. But suddenly his rocketing career stalled. He made five films within four years, each worse than the last. He hit the bottle. He found a billionaire private backer who believed in him and made a dark psychological thriller, which would be his big comeback. The film floundered for about a week then sank without a trace. He continued to maintain that though the film had flopped in America, Europe would take it to its heart. In Europe the film tanked. It wasn't even salvaged by the scandal that erupted when the backer discovered that Peppas was sleeping with his wife, and tried to strangle him. Peppas went on a talk show, ostensibly to discuss the attempt on his life, but he used the occasion to attack the great American public. He announced to the booing audience that he was abandoning America for good to take up residence in Paris, where he would make low-budget artistic films about human values, the type of films that his soul had always been longing to make, but couldn't because he had been typecast, a slave of the system.

He didn't make any films. He spent two years in Paris splashing out the last of his money on expensive hotels, expensive women and expensive drugs. Then an old friend of his, a Greek television producer, had a series that was dying in the ratings. He needed some publicity to make the public aware of it. He hired Peppas. Apart from the publicity, Peppas succeeded beyond the producer's dreams. *The Welter*, an incomprehensible drama about three brothers with multiple secrets, was transformed by Peppas as screenwriter and director into an exciting thriller that regularly topped the ratings and was now going into its fifth season. Peppas told the press that his dream from the start was to return to his beloved Greece and help, with his artistic vision, his unjustly suffering country.

"So why are you so interested?" Teri asked when she'd finished her story. "Is that prick a suspect?"

"I wish I knew," I told her.

"You know what you've done? You've sidetracked me and completely missed the point."

"And the point is…"

"That Nikos looks exactly like Sterling Hayden of course!"

Of course.

What followed was another seemingly endless monologue by Teri, but this time about Nikos Zois. I let it all wash over me, their stroll in the heart of Plaka, from the statue of Hadrian to the little alleys of Anafiotika, where Nikos analysed the Cycladic architecture of the neighbourhood while Teri looked at him in awe and could only think how to get him to bed again. I really *wanted* to seem interested. Teri was brought up by her uncle after both her parents had died of cancer a year apart while she was just a small child. Her uncle was very shy with women due to his lame leg and stayed single all his life – so Teri missed the feeling of belonging to a large family. Drag, Maria and I filled that gap. "Her brothers". That's what she called us. That's why she got in a huff when we didn't visit her. That's why she wanted to give me every detail about her "Nicky". So that she could feel that we, her family, knew everything and approved of him. So I pretended that everything I heard was of burning interest to me, while waiting for him to turn up. He phoned her to say that he was caught up in traffic – "you see how much he thinks of me?" Teri raved – and he really wasn't very late. Hearing the doorbell, Teri leapt up and rushed to the mirror three times before she was ready to open the door. When Zois came in he gave her a tender kiss and a huge bouquet of red roses. She loved them.

"You must be starving – have a seat on the sofa, I'll be right back," she told him.

She came back almost immediately carrying a plate of dainty cheese pies – her own recipe, as well. His smile seemed familiar to me, but I couldn't remember where I'd seen it before.

After he'd eaten, Teri fell asleep on his chest. I thought of what she'd told me: *Everyone has a chance, it's there, waiting for us. So why not? Why not go for it?* Watching them I wanted it to happen for them. I got up to leave, saying goodbye quietly to Zois so as not to wake Teri but she jumped up as I was going, and showed me out. She came outside with me. She trembled in the cold night air and I put my arm round her.

"So?" she whispered.

"What?"

"*What do you think of him?*"

"I've briefly met him twice. I can't give an opinion."

"First and second impression?"

"Good. Very good."

"Really?"

"He seems to be the best of the whole bunch you've made me meet."

Teri looked ready to jump for joy.

"That's what I wanted to hear! And you said a sentence of fourteen words!"

It's frightening how easy it is to make someone in love happy. And equally frightening how much it takes to please someone who isn't.

31

My next source of information was much less beautiful and much more interesting than Lena Hnara. The fact that I bothered to seek him out as early as midday impressed him – I am usually a night visitor. Omonia Square at night is like a madhouse. Never-never land. A place where anything can – and does – happen. If you have the necessary dough, of course. Or the desperate need.

I couldn't take the car. Knowing I'd never be able to park, I took the metro and emerged at the Hondos Centre, just a few steps from my source's movable house, having enjoyed one of the greatest pleasures I've had since I was a kid. I love escalators. I used to wait impatiently for that day in the month when my mum would collect whatever savings she had and take me to the Minion department store, after warning me once again that I had to behave like a little gentleman. I had a whale of a time going up and down the escalators while she would buy something cheap for me and admire all the nice stuff we could never afford. And I never misbehaved. I just let the escalators carry me along with them.

One of the hundreds of public works that had been needed for decades to make life in Athens bearable was the metro. Right from the eighties everyone knew how essential it was, and nothing was done. The government was too busy bribing voters with civil service jobs for life to fund anything else. And then, against all odds, we got to host the Olympic Games, and the metro was built with extraordinary speed. Of course, another 100 years will have to pass before it takes on the gothic romance of the London Underground, which had me captivated when I went there with Maria, years ago. I loved the astonishing variety of buskers begging for a few pennies, the combination of heat and unbearable humidity, the ceramics that portray the spirit of each station – particularly the profiles of Sherlock Holmes at Baker Street. I regarded myself as being in the same profession as Sherlock: hunting villains and bringing them to justice. That visit to London was the only time I've ever flown, overcoming, for Maria's sake, my fear of aeroplanes. With her I felt that my feet were firmly on the ground.

My Omonia source was Angelino, an ageless guy who has lived for ten years in the square, where everybody knows him. When you get to talk to him, you understand that he has about him something of the wisdom of the twenty-five centuries that look down on the city from the Acropolis. He has spent all these years living as a down-and-out when he could be living like a king. That doesn't concern him. What does is that all those who know him show their respect. As I did, nodding to him and stroking Hector, his huge German shepherd.

This skinny, grey-haired man, who won't make any impression on you if you don't look him in the eye to see how alert he is to everything that's going on, is your best bet if you want to learn the city's secrets. Nobody is so well informed about everything that takes place anywhere in Athens as Angelino. Some ignorant council workers once tried to evict him, bundling together his stuff and pushing him into a government-run home. He walked out, the council took him back, he simply walked out again. This wasn't repeated a third time; people with influence talked to the authorities and made it plain that Angelino should stay where he chose. I don't just have a business relationship with him, as do many others who pay him for the information they need. Angelino had looked after my mother when she lost her mind and started to wander the streets. I spent a lot of my time as a teenager going around different hostels and shelters trying to find her, often returning at dawn to an empty house, which would stay that way for days. I never lost my temper with her when she turned up again. She had given me such a great childhood that just remembering it made the house seem less empty. Every time I managed to find her and get through her blank, lost expression for long enough to persuade her to wrap herself up in the warm clothes I had brought her, and come back home with me, I felt that I was returning one moment of warmth for all the thousands she had given me. I felt like a man. The head of the family in the place of my absent father – Mum never wanted to talk about him and I never insisted on knowing about someone that was missing without me missing him. If it hadn't been for my mother's dementia, maybe I would never have got involved in this job and Greece would have lost its finest caretaker. I would never have risked breaking her heart by getting arrested for what people call criminal activity. But, in the end, she succumbed to the mysterious virus that had already destroyed the minds of her mother and sister. During her last difficult five years, Angelino was always there for her. Because she was, in his words, "a remarkable lady". Many times he tracked her down through his network of contacts. I would often find her playing cards with him on the pavement of the square, surrounded by cardboard boxes to screen them from passers-by. At the end she couldn't tell us apart, calling us both "my child". There couldn't have been a better way of making me feel that he was my brother.

However, brotherhood was one thing, friendship another. I was never friends with Angelino, because it was not what he wanted. He keeps people at a distance to make sure he'll survive. When I ask for information, he names the price and I pay him. But he knows how I feel; whatever he needs from me he can have.

I had called him the previous day and asked him to find out about the Bulgarian motorcyclist who tried to kill Aliki. As he started telling me what he had discovered, I watched Jordanis playing with Hector. Jordanis is the ten-year-old Albanian that Angelino unofficially adopted, sending him to the best private schools in Athens. Two years ago, after a bank robbery in which a policeman was seriously wounded, and after getting a lot of false information, the police raided the shack in Ilioupouli where the ten members of Jordanis' family lived. As the police found out the following day, the robbery had actually been done by Greeks whose leader was the son of an MP. But none of the family had residents' permits and, after interrogation, nine of them were arrested and summarily deported from the country. The tenth was

Jordanis, who, on the day of the arrests, had disobeyed his mother's orders and stayed out late playing football at a school playground. So the child was left on his own in a strange country – his parents were recent arrivals and didn't even know enough Greek to explain that they had another child there. As their confession had been beaten out of them, they didn't dare say a thing. Drag learnt all this when he questioned some of his "co-workers", as he calls them through gritted teeth.

"There's one more thing I need," I told Angelino when he had finished telling me about the Bulgarian.

"Go ahead."

"Hermes Peppas, the TV director. Do you know him, or anyone who does?"

Angelino smiled, with that grin of his that you can never decipher.

"I know him."

"Personally?"

"You could say so."

"I've found out that he's staying at the Hilton, but he's difficult to get in touch with."

"Yes, you have to be one of those arty-farty people. Or a cop. Or…"

"Or…?"

"Or I could give you a reference. Which will lighten your wallet by another five thou."

"What kind of reference?"

"You know how it goes; first you agree then I explain."

"I agree."

"Tell him I sent you. That this way he's paying me back."

"That's the reference?"

"It's enough."

"I'll get the money to you next week."

Angelino sent me. This is how you pay him back – 5,000 euros for ten words. Plus another 10,000 for the information on the Bulgarian. Knowledge is always a great source of power but Angelino had started to charge at Brazilian inflation rates. And the financial crisis only seemed to jack up his prices at a faster rate than supermarkets and hotels in Santorini. Oligarch.

"Before I leave, can you tell me why this place smells like The Body Shop?" I asked him.

"Gaultier's latest. Good, eh? My friends have showered me with presents."

"Very nice."

"I wish I could say the same about your beard."

He was right. It was awful, and it was already itching. Before I could think of something smart to say, my mobile rang. It was Drag. He asked me where I was and said that he was coming to pick me up since I didn't have a car. They still hadn't found Vassilis Stathopoulos, he told me. But they had found someone else. Dead, with a bullet in his head. Aliki's trusted psychologist, Antonis Rizos.

32

People are not equal even in death. A well-known corpse remains more important than an unknown one. And if you were to add to the well-known corpses of Dalla and Rizos the suddenly notorious corpse of Makis and the disappearance of people as celebrated as Aliki and Stathopoulos, the case was starting to feel like a noose around Drag's neck. A noose he was unable to unknot.

Drag reached Omonia Square in less than half an hour. He saw that I was with Angelino, and Angelino saw him. They gave a slight nod to each other and looked away. Angelino has a high opinion of Drag – he's a fan of gifted people who work hard to develop their talents. Drag is also sympathetic to Angelino. But he has made it clear that if he finds him mixed up in a case that he is handling, Drag won't hesitate to find him a nice prison bed. I happened to be present when they had that conversation. Angelino listened quietly to Drag, then turned away to watch the sun setting over the jagged Athens skyline. And he stood there gazing at the sunset until we left. Since then they just nod at each other, barely acknowledging each other's existence.

I said goodbye to Angelino and got into Drag's Nissan. He was in a foul temper and looked as if he hadn't slept for days. He'd interviewed the investigators that Stathopoulos had hired, been through the police records of everyone involved in the story, questioned the cast members of the TV series in which Dalla and Aliki co-starred as well as Stathopoulos' lawyers, and raided a TV production company, where the owner, a thirty-year-old swindler, was hiding. This swindler had been heard to say he would kill both Vassilis and Aliki after Aliki had turned down his offer to make another series, but it soon became clear that he was really in hiding from the father of some kid he'd knocked up. Dozens of actors and actresses who had had a nodding relationship with Aliki had also passed through Drag's office. Most of them arrived voluntarily, all dolled up for the paparazzi, and, of course, their testimony contributed no new information whatever.

But Drag did have two lucky breaks. He first found Makis' best friend, Vaggos. Once he had his name it wasn't difficult, since Vaggos was in jail. He had been arrested for drink-driving, with performance-enhancing drugs in the back of his car. Vaggos, who stated his profession to be "personal trainer", had claimed that the stuff was purely for personal use. Seeing there were four suitcases packed with the stuff, the judge hadn't been convinced. Drag offered Vaggos a deal, if he could tell him something useful about Makis. He did and he didn't. He said that Makis had boasted about fucking the brains out of a rich bitch he'd fallen in love with, after which he had cut himself off from all his friends. Not even Vaggos had been able to get near him recently. Drag's second break was a phone call from a secretary who had been sacked by Rizos. She told him she was certain that the relationship between her former boss and Aliki was much more than purely professional. It seemed that, after all, Makis was not the only one with a strong personal interest in the case, as the late therapist had claimed.

Drag's luck didn't last long. An hour after he'd found out about Rizos' relationship with Aliki, the therapist's body was discovered by his new secretary. He had asked her to pick up some files; she found his door open, went in and there he was, holding the gun that had killed him. There was no note, which Drag explained by saying it wasn't a suicide. "They're running more checks in the lab, but Rizos was shot from a distance. The bullet only penetrated a couple of inches into his head, which means it couldn't have been fired from up close," Drag said.

"Could the killer have been somewhere outside the house?"

"Impossible. The windows on one side face a wall; on the other they look onto a flat that was full of people."

"Meaning he was killed somewhere else."

"Mmm... Must have walked into an ambush and then they brought him back to make it look like suicide."

"Time of death?"

"Sometime yesterday; the pathologist can't say exactly when yet."

"So, Makis goes to Rizos' office to get information from him any way he can. Rizos survives that, only to be killed a day later. But not by Makis, as he was dead by then. Are you thinking what I'm thinking?"

"The way your mind works, I doubt it," he replied.

I gave him a look. He produced a grimace that vaguely resembled a smile.

"You're thinking that our friend Vassilis is behind all this," he said.

I nodded.

"Remember what he told us about Rizos, the first time we went to his house? '*She met him quite often. Maybe too often*'," I said.

"So maybe Vassilis suspected or knew about Rizos' affair with Aliki. Maybe he sent Makis to kill Rizos, not just get information out of him."

"And then what? He killed Makis in that theatrical manner and did the job on Rizos himself?" I asked. That made no sense to me.

"If it was Aliki who Makis was having an affair with…"

"You think she was screwing Rizos as well as Makis?"

"What, she's too much of a lady for that?"

"But with *Makis*?" I insisted.

I could see her with Rizos. He was much older, yes, but a father figure who was helping her sort herself out. But Makis had nothing to offer her. Unless…

"Maybe she wanted to get him to kill Vassilis. He was right there, at his side every day; it would be easier for him than anyone else," Drag said, articulating my thoughts exactly. That could be the reason why Makis hadn't told Vassilis about Aliki being at the fast-food joint. Maybe he wanted to find her for himself. Maybe he wasn't a hired gun looking to bring his boss's wife back home, but a disgruntled lover. Which would give her extra reasons to flee, as she did.

"But why didn't Makis kill him, then? If he had the motive and the opportunity, why didn't he? Why did she have to come to me, a stranger?"

"Perhaps she couldn't persuade him. She might not be that good in bed," Drag said, although it was obvious he didn't believe what he was saying even as he was saying it. He tried another tack.

"Or maybe he did try to kill Vassilis. Maybe he tried yesterday, failed – not rare for him – and Vassilis killed him instead."

"And hanged him from the chandelier? Why?"

"Because he found out Makis was sleeping with his wife. If he's half as crazy as Aliki claims, it would be reason enough. Maybe Makis told him that Rizos was sleeping with Aliki as well. So he killed Makis and then went straight to deal with Rizos."

"What about the hieroglyphs?" I asked him.

"If I had all the unpleasant answers, I'd be minister of finance," he replied.

The trouble was, his theory wouldn't hold water if the "rich bitch" sleeping with Makis wasn't Aliki. Lena, maybe? No. She'd never get *involved* with someone like Makis. Vassilis did indeed seem to be our prime suspect. He hadn't told us about his affair with Elsa. He was obviously lying when he said he didn't care about Aliki's past, and Lena had seen him behaving like a psychotic bully towards his wife. He had a motive to kill Rizos, a possible motive to kill Makis and, besides, who else could have been at his house killing Makis and leaving the door open for us to find the body? But why open the door? To taunt us, show us we can't catch him? However much he lied to me, Vassilis seemed too organized, too much of a control freak to go on a murder spree like this.

I still had questions that could only be answered when, or if, we found Aliki and Vassilis. But Vassilis wasn't the only one that had lied to us. I didn't tell Drag what Lena had told me about Aliki and Hermes Peppas, about the director's failure to remember, during Drag's interrogation, that he and Aliki had been lovers. I was paying Angelino through the nose for the chance to talk to Peppas face to face, and I wasn't going to miss it. Apart from that, I always had one basic advantage over Drag: I wasn't accountable to anyone for my behaviour, especially if I discovered that someone was hiding information from me.

Drag wrenched the steering wheel and overtook three cars. Two of the drivers gave him the finger, while the third let out a stream of abuse.

"What did Angelino tell you?"

I gave Drag the names and addresses of the family of the Bulgarian who had been killed trying to murder Aliki. The police hadn't even found out his name, though it had been child's play for Angelino. He told me the Bulgarian's parents and brothers worked legally and hard and had had no involvement with the police, nor did they want to. They were expecting to get their residence permits any day, which is why they hadn't gone to the police to declare their relationship to the deceased, when they learnt what he had done. He was the black sheep of the family, and they didn't want to endanger their future in their new country by becoming known as the relatives of a criminal. Only after months had passed and they had made certain that the graveyard wasn't under police surveillance did the mother start to go, once a month, to light a candle over her son's unmarked grave. Immigrants are like soldiers – they can only look forward to the next battle, they often don't even get the chance to bury their dead. They would probably tell Drag everything they knew, however upset they might be. As long as he didn't go in a police car, of course – they were living in St Panteleimonas, in the heart of Athens where if you see a policeman you just run – and he would have to reassure them that their permits wouldn't be at risk.

Drag gave me a look, when I told him where in Acharnon Street he would find their house. Just a week earlier, we'd seen an Afghan woman there, calling in vain for someone to help her son who lay dying in the middle of the road, covered in blood. At St Pantelcimonas everybody minds their own business. St Panteleimonas. The saint who has mercy on everybody. An area named by a godfather with a great sense of irony. Drag had put the siren on his car and kept his hand on the horn during the whole ride to the hospital, but the doctors hadn't been able to save the kid. In the waiting room the mother kept looking at me, without speaking, with that insurmountable grief of those who keep staring disaster in the face. When Drag talked to his fellow cops of the Acharnon police department about the kid, they said, "we'll check it out". They never do. Why should they put their lives at risk for 1,000 euros per month when they are constantly understaffed? They know that they will always be surrounded by the immigrants' shit on the train lines, by the gangs who run the area and are at constant war with each other, by the protesting Greeks who, instead of leaving for more fashionable neighbourhoods like so many others did, insist on living where they grew up. Although they feel like foreigners in their own country and are scared for their lives. Now St Panteleimonas is filled with Bulgarian shops and grocery stores. They do much better business than the Greek ones, because they speak the same language as their customers.

It took us three quarters of an hour to get to my place. We had already agreed what exactly each of us would do next. Aliki's and Vassilis' mobiles were still turned off. I opened the Nissan's passenger door and froze. Drag never comes into the house in case he meets Maria, and the one time he breaks that rule, there she is right in front of us. She had just come out of the house, wearing jeans and a sweater, with little make-up, her hair loose and her deep green eyes trained on us. Drag, sitting next to me, seemed to have gone paler than my targets, when they see me and suddenly realize that their lives are about to end. I wasn't doing much better than Drag. We were both paralysed. Until Maria started to walk towards the car quite normally. She stopped by my window.

"Hi there," she said.

"Hi," Drag said.

"Hi," I echoed.

"Aren't you going to ask me to get in?" she asked.

I turned and stared at Drag. He stayed silent.

"I was just about to get out..." I said, trying to save the situation.

"Of course, get in," Drag said, breaking into one of his rare grins, before I could continue.

"Shall we go for a drive so that you can tell me your news?" Maria said, once she had got in, and for a moment I felt that we were teenagers again, all together at school. As though not a day had passed.

It turned out Maria was actually going to Teri's house, to talk about Nikos Zois. Drag, who became more and more relaxed, drove us there, and they started to talk. As though not a day had passed. Occasionally I would chip in, mainly on the subject of Nikos, since I was the only one to have met him. But mostly I just looked at them. I felt like I had left my body and was watching from far away as the woman of my dreams and my best friend talked to forget the fact they couldn't make each other happy. Like in a movie, I somehow hoped that they would end up together.

We got snarled up in traffic, so it took us an hour to get to Galatsi. Drawn up outside Teri's house, none of us could stop talking. We wanted to keep hold of the moment forever. Finally, Maria said: "I should be going." And, before we managed to answer, she caressed both our faces, whispering: "Be very careful, for my sake", and got out of the car.

On our silent journey back to the house, Athens was covered by a mass of huge black clouds. The weathermen had forecast a deluge but it didn't materialize. Instead there was a stifling, damp heat that kept the rain at bay, and stopped it washing away everything we couldn't bear to think about.

33

I hurried into the Hilton and went towards the reception desk with the intention of asking them to put me through to Peppas' room. I was sure that the answer they would give me would be the same as if I had phoned: that Mr Peppas had a list of people he would talk to, and if I gave them my name, they would check if I was on it. Like any star, he took precautions to safeguard his privacy; as for living in a hotel, he'd told one interviewer that houses need a lot of tidying and he doesn't have time to waste on such trivial things.

I was about to introduce myself to the concierge as Angelino, when I saw Peppas, some distance away, dressed in a bathrobe and accompanied by a fat guy in a suit, with an enormous head, going towards the solarium. There's no better time than winter to get a tan. I went into the Hilton's coffee bar, and took a seat from which I could see Peppas on his return from tanning. After exactly one hour, he reappeared, accompanied by his friend who reminded me of Oddjob, the murderous Asian with the guillotine bowler hat in *Goldfinger*. I had already paid for my coffee, which was good but not worth what they charged for it, and darted towards them. Luckily, they were walking slowly, and talking animatedly.

"Mr Peppas?" I said.

"Just a lookalike," he answered, turning his back.

Very funny. "Mr Peppas…"

"Leave us alone, man, will you? He doesn't give autographs," the other guy butted in. His eyes were like buttonholes in a sea of fat. Taking Peppas by the arm, he led him away to continue their conversation.

"Angelino sent me," I said.

Peppas turned and looked at me.

"Who?"

"Angelino. He said that you'd answer a few of my questions and that's how you'll pay him back."

He asked me to follow him to his suite.

Once there, I discovered from their conversation about some new contract that the fat guy was Labis Louridis, Peppas' manager. He was about to leave for Thessaloniki to finalize the deal they were discussing, and it was obvious he didn't approve of my presence. I pretended not to notice, and gazed at the Parthenon, which was directly opposite the window. For a few minutes it was bathed in the light of a sun that quickly disappeared, dispelling hopes of a change in the weather. I was lucky that the haze was thin enough to allow me even a glimpse of the temple.

The window offered the only view of the real world. The suite was full of screens, innumerable TVs on which a variety of Greek and foreign channels were playing.

"Oof! Got rid of him!" exclaimed Peppas as soon as Louridis left.

"I thought stars had good relationships with their managers," I said.

He smiled on hearing the word "star". It was probably enough to make him ignore the rest of my sentence. "Labis is OK, poor guy, but I want to relax a bit, to be on my own, to *cultivate my inner self*, but he doesn't leave me in peace, he's so... what's the word I'm looking for?"

"Overprotective?"

"Yes, yes, that's it. And he *stifles* me," he said, fanning himself with the contract and glancing round at the screens. It was a while before he remembered I was still there. "So, you know Angelino, do you?"

"Yes."

"Friends?"

"You could put it that way."

"A good man, Angelino. On the level. What do you want to ask me?"

"About your relationship with Aliki Stylianou."

That took him by surprise. He didn't speak for a few seconds.

"How do you know about that?"

Not from Drag, anyhow, since you forgot to mention it to him, I thought.

"Do you need to know?" I asked.

"I don't *need* to, but..."

"Then you don't."

"Will you tell me why you're interested, at least?"

"Let's say I'm looking into the case."

"Not a cop, eh?"

"No."

"Then what? A detective?"

"Something like that."

"And you're looking into the case? *Great!* Let me ask you, while we're talking, would it bother you if I film it? You see, I'm writing a screenplay with a detective as the lead… I have to write it myself, all the scripts they send me are such rubbish – and I want to know how people on the job really behave."

"It would."

"What?"

"Bother me."

"Oh. I can pay you, if you want."

"I don't want."

"Fine. OK. Just let me get some water…"

He went to the kitchen and came back with two glasses of water, one of which he offered me. Then he sat down and got out a spotless white handkerchief from his dressing gown, with which he proceeded to wipe each one of his fingers with great thoroughness. Seeing me looking, he said, "I have a bit of a phobia of germs."

"That must make your life difficult," I said.

"Not if I am careful. Which I am, about everything."

He continued to wipe his hands, and then said, "Are you sure you don't want me to film you?"

"Very flattering, but no."

"I am only really at ease when I'm surrounded by cameras, understand? It would make it easier for me to answer your questions."

"Alright," I agreed, seeing that we were getting nowhere. "*Wonderful!*"

He folded his handkerchief and put it in his pocket. Then he opened a cupboard and took out a video camera.

"Don't worry, I won't show it to anyone, it's just for me."

"I hope so."

"Really!"

"Tell me about Aliki."

He pressed the "record" button and a red light flashed. As he spoke he moved around, shooting me from different angles. I wondered if he found me photogenic.

"Aliki… The darkest and brightest kid I've ever known," he said.

"Meaning?"

"I don't have to explain the bright side, you'd have to be blind not to… see it. She seems to light up… any place she visits."

His dialogue was fractured as he concentrated on getting the shots he wanted.

"And, as an actress… she has a big future ahead… her looks… persistence… we just have to find her, make sure she's safe… had to make some changes… the script. You know, sending her on holiday… usual thing… Any idea where she is?"

"Nothing yet. What about her dark side?"

Peppas stopped his restless moving and kept the camera on my face.

"You don't see it unless you spend a lot of time with her. And when you've seen it, you don't want to see it again. At least, I didn't, which is why I let her slip away from me. I remember her stopping while we were talking and looking at me with such intensity my hair stood on end. As if she'd never looked at me before… as if she wanted to devour me. Her voice didn't change, but that look… As if her face couldn't cope with what she was thinking… Whenever I tried to ask her about her past, she'd give me vague evasive answers, but she managed me in the way she knew best. In bed. Her great talent. Only it was too wild for me, I don't know if you follow me…?"

"I'm trying."

"Relationships with actresses I've had… even I don't know how many. And not, of course, because they love my hairy belly. They try and disguise it, but they're all hoping for a break. I've never before had a first date like the one I had with Aliki. We didn't bother with coffee or something to eat but went straight to my room in the hotel. And then she asked me where I'd like to come on her."

I remembered Drag who, when he hears of such women, says, "In my village we call them slags," and I answer, "Drag, you haven't got a village", and he says: "Yes, but I'd like to have one."

"Any chance she wanted you with an ungovernable passion?" I asked him.

"None. I asked her if she wouldn't like a fairy-tale romance, complete with happy ending with the two of us disappearing hand-in-hand into the sunset. And she said, 'I don't need any more – I've had enough in my life.'"

"What did she mean?"

"I don't know. Never found out. Never cared to find out, to tell you the truth – I had already decided that we had no future together, especially after I discovered that she liked… something more violent. I'm a bit traditional about such things."

"When you say violent…"

"Both doing and having it done to her."

"Including, let's say, cutting with knives?"

"Cutting, hitting, whips, clubs, knives and other things I didn't even know could give pleasure. She is one of those women who can make you feel ignorant in bed."

Until that moment, the explanations for Aliki's scars were that either she inflicted them on herself or that they were caused by her husband. Now it looked as if they had both lied, and the scars were the result of their idea of a good time together.

"So, it ended up with her driving me wild with regular sex, and me avoiding the madness that drove her wild," Peppas continued.

"But you stayed together for nine months."

"It was less than three. I decided that I wasn't interested in getting her to trust me and confide all her dark secrets. She wasn't happy with me, I wasn't happy seeing her not happy... Sometimes you reach a critical point where you ask yourself whether you really want to get to know the other person better. I didn't. I didn't even know myself well then, I hadn't read the *I Ching*, so how could I be interested in others? Do you know about the *I Ching*?" he asked.

"Eh... no," I said.

If people think you're ignorant, the intelligent person lets them continue to think so.

"It's one of the most ancient Chinese texts. Cosmology and philosophy. Hexagrams explaining the workings of fortune. Acceptance of the forces of change in the universe."

The way he explained it, even I, who knew about it, found it difficult to understand.

"Is this relevant to our discussion?"

"Not exactly. But the *I Ching* explains everything, so it could explain how we two unique beings happen to find ourselves talking together in this room. And if I had read it then, I may have paid more attention to Aliki. To lead her out of her darkness, instead of letting her get mixed up with that…"

"Who do you mean?"

"The man's a friend of mine – loosely speaking. But he suffers from a complete lack of spirituality, while I have been going through a cleansing process for some time now. Both spiritual and physical. I've decided that I don't want to hide any secrets from anyone, not even myself. While he continues to do anything and everything for money."

"Who?"

"I'll show you."

He went to a massive desk and opened a drawer. He shuffled through some photos and passed one of them to me.

"Now I'm off the coke completely. That evening, with them, was one of the last times. I was almost clean then but they persuaded me and we posed for the photo thinking that we were doing something fun."

"Is that who I think it is?"

"It's him alright."

In the photograph with him and Aliki was Takis Vrettos. Famous since his early twenties for the profits he made as a student during the crazy Greek stock market boom. Even more famous because, after a series of high-ranking positions, he became president of Omikron, led it to become the number one private bank investing in hedge funds, quit shortly after the crisis started and bought the bank soon afterwards for one tenth of its actual worth, on behalf of a German corporation. Now he was running it again. Unlike Peppas, Vrettos' career didn't have ups and downs. The only way for this particular golden boy seemed to be up.

"I'm not at all proud to show this to you," Peppas said.

All three of them were naked, with Aliki between them looking alluringly at the camera while Peppas and Vrettos were bent down on each side of her, licking her breasts.

"After that evening, I told her I didn't want to carry on."

"Why?"

"Because when I woke up alone in bed the next morning – the two of them had cleared off – when I saw the photos and how my eyes looked, I decided I didn't want another catastrophe in my life when I was becoming successful again. That was when I started my purification."

"How did Aliki take that?"

"Our separation? She was cool. Very cool, with that 'coolness' that is close to 'cold'. Besides, from the moment I introduced them, Aliki got on much better with Takis than she'd ever done with me. Maybe they were already sleeping together before that photo session. Maybe our threesome was planned as a farewell performance. I don't know. I don't care."

"How long were Aliki and Takis together?"

"Not long, I think. Longer than her and me, but it was only a matter of months before she got to know her husband."

Lena Hnara had told me that Aliki's relationship with Peppas had lasted eight or nine months. Which meant that Aliki had completely omitted to mention her relationship with Takis to her best friend, leaving her to believe that she was still with Peppas.

"Do you know Vassilis Stathopoulos?" I asked him.

Vassilis, Aliki, her former lovers... I was violating my own rules and mentioning names. But it didn't seem like a problem. Not only had I still not finally decided on my target, also I was hearing such contradictory things about them there wasn't any chance of my feeling involved.

"No, not at all," Peppas said. "Just a wave or a handshake when we happened to meet in public. Aliki was always very happy to see me at the few parties I attend…"

"Did Vassilis ever seem annoyed that she was so pleased to see you?"

"I never noticed anything like that. He didn't seem to know about us, but if he did and it annoyed him, would he have shown it?"

Good question. And, as with dozens of others, I had no answer.

"Do you want this? Maybe you'll need it," said Peppas, holding out the photograph.

"Aren't you worried I might circulate it?"

"Angelino phoned me while I was down in the pool. He told me that someone would come looking for me and that he was completely reliable; one of his guys. Those were exactly his words. He asked me to tell you whatever you need to know – and not to fear that anything I say could be used against me. I like that. It's also part of my cleansing, not to hold anything back."

The 5,000 I gave Angelino had been a worthwhile investment, after all.

"Take the photo. Takis, if he doesn't know you, won't even admit that two plus two equals four. Maybe the photo will help persuade him to talk – if you can find him, of course."

"Why? Where is he?"

"In rehab – as if he'll ever drop the habit, but there he is, anyway."

"Which clinic?"

He didn't know. I had only a few questions left.

"Did you have a good relationship with Elsa Dalla?"

"Not really. It wasn't the poor girl's fault – I was very upset when I heard about her... Tragedy, tragedy... So young... It was our producer's fault. Regoudis. An idiot and a half, like most producers. Some girl falls to her knees in front of them and suddenly they're inspired. They think they've discovered a new Ava Gardner. The girl was OK, tried to do her job. Tried, as hard as she could."

"Untalented?"

"Very untalented, sadly. She managed not to make a fool of herself in front of the cameras, but that's as far as it went. Very beautiful, of course, very, very... but you know, even beauty, for certain people... if you're not star quality, beauty makes things worse. It deprives you of an excuse. Why are you failing, if you look like that?"

"Did she have anything to do with Aliki?"

"Not as far as I know. I never saw them together."

"Was there maybe animosity between them?"

"Animosity? No, why would there be?"

"Because Elsa and Stathopoulos, Aliki's husband, used to be an item."

He looked at me, surprised – unless he was putting on an act.

"You're kidding me... I had no idea. But, animosity... no, not at all. Elsa... she liked being on her own, she had her own personal dressing room at the studio and her own trailer on location – provided by Regoudis, so that she could feel like a real leading lady. All the time we weren't shooting she'd be in there, alone; she didn't really have any friends in the cast."

"But she *did* resemble Aliki a lot."

"Mmm... I wouldn't agree. Does a Picasso look like its copy? Does the sea look like a big lake?"

"Depends who is looking at them," I said.

"Right. You're absolutely right! So yes, I guess if you put them side-by-side they looked alike. Actually, now that you mention it, in an episode where Aliki had a monologue, looking at herself in the mirror, Elsa came and suggested that she could wear a wig and different make-up so that I could shoot from the side, having Aliki talk to her instead of the mirror. I lied, told her that I didn't like the idea artistically. It wasn't really a bad idea, but the public wouldn't buy it for a second. Aliki makes any woman look inferior, even more so if the woman looks something like her. The difference would have been so clear, we would have been a laughing stock."

"So, no animosity. But no closeness either?"

"No."

"You don't think they appreciated each other's beauty?"

"I can't even remember them looking at each other for more than a few seconds."

"OK. Speaking of photos, do you know this guy?" I asked him, and showed him the picture of Linesman from my phone. I had cropped it, cutting out Aliki and Elsa.

"Funny-looking guy. No, I don't know him. But I could use him for a small role in the series – do you know where I can find him?"

Actually, I did.

"I'm afraid he's unavailable. Do you know if either Aliki or Elsa had any knowledge of Ancient Egypt or the Mayan civilization?"

"You're talking about the hieroglyphics they found on that bodyguard…? No, not to my knowledge. Of course, I didn't know much about Elsa, but Aliki can't speak any foreign languages. That's not her cup of tea."

"I've worked out that much. Anyone else that might know anything useful about them?"

"I can't think of… well, there's one person that they both spent a lot of time with. Their hair stylist. They both loved that girl's work."

"What's her name?"

"Torrence. Samantha Torrence. English name, but she's Greek."

I managed not to smile when I heard her name.

After so many dead ends, Peppas had given me one good lead to Takis Vrettos and a reason to visit someone I knew well and liked very much. What Peppas told me had the ring of truth about it. I thanked him and stood up.

"May I just have another glass of water?" I asked.

"Yes, of course. Aliki and Elsa with Stathopoulos, eh? I had no idea…"

He put down his camera on the chair, got out his handkerchief and went to the kitchen, wiping his fingers. I heard the tap running.

By the time he'd returned I'd pressed the delete button on the camera and was on my way to the lift. For his own good I hoped that he had actually told me the truth; that I wouldn't have to go back and see him again.

34

I didn't expect much from visiting Sam, but I had some free time while Drag found out which rehab clinic Takis Vrettos was in. We'd agreed that I would go, since it would take too much effort for Drag to get a warrant to question patients in a clinic, and we didn't even know if Takis had anything that would help clear up our case.

Sam hadn't changed a bit, in the four years since I'd seen her. I used to visit that apartment often, to see Jackie, Samantha's sister, when they lived together. Sam always made sure Jackie and I would be alone, so I rarely saw her and when I did she always made an excuse and left. For some reason she believed that I would be able to persuade her sister to stay in Greece. I wasn't. Jackie and I had a good time together, but it was clear to both of us that it was nothing more than that. We weren't in love. I never thought that Jackie was one of the three women that would make their mark on me, as per *A Bronx Tale*. Plus, our work didn't exactly favour romance, me being a caretaker whose targets were confined to Greece, Jackie working for the British Foreign Office in embassies all over the world while actually being a spy for MI6. We got to know each other on the job. I had agreed to take care of Morton, a colleague of hers she was investigating as a possible double agent, who profited by selling information to Arab extremist organizations. I was working for Morton's cousin, who had discovered he was sexually abusing her teenage daughter. Jackie wasn't happy that I killed Morton before she had amassed enough evidence to arrest him, but that didn't stop her from joining me in bed. We only stayed together for a few months, in a relationship with plenty of animal attraction and few words – Jackie was even more taciturn than I was.

"It's lovely to see you again," Sam said, hugging me at the door. Unlike her sister, who had inherited the Mediterranean characteristics of their Greek mother, Sam had her father's pale complexion, which always made her seem vulnerable.

"Are you still working out?" she asked as she touched my arm, but before I could reply she led me into the living room, where cups of coffee and a plate of biscuits and chocolates were waiting.

"How's Jackie?" I asked, more because I knew it was the right thing to say than because I really cared.

"In her own words, she's never had more fun. That's what she emailed last week from China. I really don't know just what she enjoys in that job of hers."

I wasn't sure that she knew exactly what her sister's job was. Jackie swore that she didn't, because she'd only worry all the time. So I changed the subject.

"I see you've made a few changes to the place."

She laughed.

"That's a hell of an understatement," she said.

She had turned the two-bedroom apartment into a professional hair salon.

"You still working for TV and movies?" I asked.

"When there's a job. Which becomes rarer and rarer. I've only got one TV series now, and I'm lucky to get even that. You know most TV stations will be forced to close, now that only four public channels are allowed in the whole country."

I nodded.

"And movies were always an extreme sport in Greece. So here I am."

She opened her hands as if to embrace the apartment.

"Nice," I said, though I wasn't being entirely sincere.

Our knees were touching and there was something in the way she kept looking at me and had grabbed my arm... The memories from the apartment were giving me ideas I shouldn't have.

"Not really nice, but it was the best I could do. I don't pay any rent, as the apartment is mine, or any tax – I'm supposedly only living here. I'm not going to pay those bastards two thirds of my income to get nothing back for my taxes."

"Still, if someone tells on you..."

"I'll find a way to sue them for misconduct and the case will be in the courts for a decade. But you aren't here to talk about me and tax evasion, are you?"

"No."

She moved a little away from me and crossed her legs.

"As I told you on the phone, I'm helping out a friend who's looking into the Aliki Stylianou case," I said.

Jackie had mentioned to Sam that I was working in private law enforcement. Which was close to the truth if you substituted "justice" for "law".

"That can't be fun," she said. "I've been following the news, like, hourly. Poor Elsa… and everyone's speculating about Aliki and her husband… What's really going on?"

"I'll be glad to tell you when I find out myself. I know from Hermes Peppas that you were the hair stylist to both Aliki and Elsa, and they loved your work."

"Well… I'm good, if I say so myself," she smiled.

Her smile lit up her face and made her nose seem less pointed.

"Anything weird that you might have noticed in their behaviour?"

"You mean towards each other?"

"And on their own."

"I'd seldom see them speak to each other; they barely said 'hi'. I'd go as far as saying they deliberately ignored each other – but that's common in TV, actresses often act weird around one another."

Unless they're lovers and want to hide it from everybody.

"But it's not like they met often. Elsa kept getting bigger and bigger scenes to play and was in her trailer with her acting coach, or talking to Regoudis, her sugar daddy. Aliki just comes for a few takes, does her scenes and leaves. Other than that, what else can I tell you…? They had different attitudes. Aliki doesn't really care much about how she'll appear on screen; whatever I do with her hair she knows she'll look like a goddess, so she's all about the acting, she loves it even if it's a one-minute scene."

"Elsa didn't enjoy it?"

"Not that much. I think she loved being in the spot-light more. She had to be perfectly groomed before even leaving her trailer. Wasn't too difficult, of course, the way she looked, but she was more peculiar… God, I'm saying 'was' and I still can't believe she's gone."

"Did you like them?"

"As clients?"

"As people."

"Reasonably. Didn't have any problems with them, but didn't become friends either."

"Anything peculiar that you may have noticed? Some phone call that you happened to overhear, something they said?"

"Not really."

"Someone you saw them with and seemed strange, who had no reason to be there? Like this guy?" I showed her the photo of Linesman.

"I've never seen him before."

"How about this one? He worked as Aliki's bodyguard," I said, and showed her a picture of Makis.

"He's the one…"

She meant "the one that was murdered". I nodded.

"I'd seen him waiting for her, a few times. She was very friendly towards him."

"Perhaps too friendly?"

"You mean… I don't know, I'm not sure about that. Aliki has a very flirtatious manner, the way she talks anyone might think she's coming on to them, but she isn't, it's just her way of speaking, moving…"

I knew what she meant.

"It doesn't mean she's sleeping with everyone she's friendly with," Sam said.

I wasn't too sure about that, based on the information I'd recently gathered.

"For example, she wasn't more friendly with him than with her other bodyguard," Sam continued.

"What other bodyguard?"

"There were two of them, the one you showed me and a very good-looking one. Some days one would come to get her, some days the other."

"Do you remember his name?"

"No, I never spoke to him, or heard him speak. I once tried to attract his attention, but no luck, he was all business," she said, and smiled mischievously.

A second bodyguard. If Vassilis was the killer, he must have had help, both for Elsa's murder – as he was highly unlikely to shoot someone in the middle of the road – and for hanging Makis on the chandelier.

A second bodyguard, which Vassilis had neglected to mention, just like he had neglected to tell us about his affair with Elsa. I ate a couple of cocoa- and hazelnut-filled wafers. I thought that maybe I should stay there, spend my time eating biscuits and letting Sam stroke my arm. Maybe inertia was the secret of a happy life.

If it was, I wasn't yet ready to embrace it.

35

I called Drag, gave him Sam's number and told him she was expecting his call if he thought she should see a police sketch artist to describe the second bodyguard. The description she gave me could fit thousands of Athenians.

Drag had some news from his end.

"Remember Tolis?" he asked me.

Tolis was a computer whiz who Drag had wanted to hire for his team for quite a while. He had gone to his boss and said he should create a job for Tolis immediately, as there was no one who was anywhere near as smart in their IT department. The chief of police had asked the minister of citizen protection, who had asked the minister of administrative reform, who has asked the minister of finance, who had asked the prime minister, who had asked the representatives of the Quartet. But before Tolis' salary became a matter for endless negotiation between the European Central Bank, the IMF, the European Commission and the European Stability Mechanism, Drag found a millionaire whose name he'd once cleared to fund the new post.

"I remember Tolis," I said.

"He managed to find who had posted the photo Maria came up with, with Elsa, Aliki and Linesman."

"And?"

"We've got him here, at headquarters. Fifties, gay-hater, lives with his mother. Says he can't remember when he took the photo but he recalls that Elsa and Aliki were all but fucking each other and the guy who was with them in that bar."

"Linesman?"

"Nope. He can't even remember if Linesman was in Aliki's company that night. I showed him photos of Vassilis, Makis, Regoudis, Peppas and Vrettos. Again nothing. I tried with photos of the actors from the TV series Aliki and Elsa were in. Nada. It was another guy. And our photographer can't remember the guy's features, said it was dark and all his attention was on the girls."

"If you get a decent sketch from Sam's description, show it to him and see if that jogs his memory. There's one man we're missing in every step of this story. If Vassilis is still our main suspect, we need to find the guy who must have helped him. He could be the key to everything."

Drag agreed, and in return pointed me towards the place Takis Vrettos was in rehab.

"Rehabilitation clinic". Maybe you have an image of inmates locked up in white rooms, howling like wolves as they endure the symptoms of withdrawal. Maybe you think of hollow-eyed young women dressed in rags, sweating and screaming and clawing at the walls as they go cold turkey. The place Takis was in was nothing like that.

The drive was choked with Porsches and Ferraris. Bodyguards surrounded a well-known young actor who was entwined with his girlfriend, screaming with laughter, both coked up to the eyeballs. The place looked and felt like a luxury hotel, and the staff and security dressed and behaved appropriately, treating their clients with the utmost politeness. Only someone who attempted to disturb their guests' privacy would be regarded as an unwelcome intruder.

A short, stout man with thick, black, curly hair hurried over to me, all smiles. The name-sign on his lapel read "Zissis". "Is someone looking after you, Mr…?"

"Louridis. Labis Louridis."

"Mr Louridis, how can I be of service to you?"

"I want to speak to Mr Vrettos."

"And you are…?"

"A colleague."

"Unfortunately we have strict instructions not to allow anyone to disturb him."

"He will want to see me, Zissis."

His smile never faltered as he sized me up, trying to decide whether or not to believe me. I smiled back.

"Just a minute…" he said.

I had passed the first test. He tapped at his computer to find Takis' room number, but he kept the screen hidden from me. If I'd known his room number I might have been able to make a sprint for the stairs behind the lift, which seemed to be unguarded, but I didn't want to make a scene, and I certainly didn't want another police sketch of me doing the rounds in the media, even if this one had a beard. I looked around for inspiration, taking in the deep-pile, crimson carpets, the huge marble fireplace, the tasteful sculptures and paintings on the walls, the signs for the heated swimming pool, the billiard room and the squash courts. None of them sparked an idea of how I might get to Takis if he refused to see me. Zissis was talking to him in a low voice.

"Did you say Louridis?" he asked, glancing up at me.

"Louridis, yes. I'm Hermes Peppas' manager. I want to talk to Mr Vrettos about an ad for Omikron that my client would like to direct."

Zissis conveyed my message word-for-word. Then he said "yes" several times and put the phone down. "You can go up to room 603 in ten minutes. In the meantime, if you would like to wait in our café, I'll arrange for somebody to escort you."

In the café I ordered some kind of sweet from the long list on the menu, more out of curiosity than anything, because each one cost as much as a whole meal in a normal restaurant. What arrived on my table within a few minutes wasn't enough to satisfy a half-starved sparrow, but the taste was extraordinary. It reminded me of Luisa, a work colleague of Teri's, who never stayed with a client for more than an hour. However much money she was offered for more time to enjoy her talents, her standard reply was "Next time. I'm better in small portions."

After ten minutes I returned to the reception desk. Zissis gestured to one of the security staff who was about my size, but maybe heavier. We eyed each other as he escorted me to the lift, and went up to the sixth floor in complete silence. When I knocked at room 603, the door opened but the face that met me was certainly not that of Takis Vrettos.

"Mr Louridis…" said the face.

"Good day."

"We've never met, but I've heard about you. You seem… different from the descriptions."

"Better in the flesh, I hope."

"Vanessa Ferri. I'm Takis' advisor," she said briskly, thrusting out a cool hand.

Vanessa. Advisor. She was barely twenty. Well, at least he had taste. She was tall, graceful, with huge brown eyes and blond hair tied back in a ponytail. She was wearing a designer-label suit, which failed to make her look more mature and serious.

"Come in," she said.

The suite consisted of three large rooms, the door to one of which was closed. I saw a jumble of clothes thrown on a bed as I followed Vanessa into the lounge and sat on a large sofa. Maybe she needed the ten minutes to decide what to wear.

Vanessa sat in a rocking chair, tucked one long leg under the other and started to rock herself.

"I'm listening."

She'd probably seen a film with managers in it and was trying to mimic their behaviour. "I would prefer Takis to be present."

"Takis is resting. He's come here for some peace and quiet and he's not seeing anyone. I only convey what's absolutely necessary. He is one of the most successful businessmen in this country, and we have to protect talent. You certainly understand that, having Peppas as a client."

"Mr Peppas told me to speak only with Takis. My understanding was that, because of their friendship, Takis would agree."

"Tell him to come in person, if they are such good friends. As his manager you are only entitled to speak with me. Understood?"

For a twenty-year-old she had an extremely sharp tongue. So sharp she might cut herself.

I stood up.

"Mr Peppas wants to make an ad that will completely change the image people have of banks in Greece. Everyone despises banks now, no one trusts them. We can change this. We will change this. If you're not interested, we'll go elsewhere... Good day."

"Hey, baby!"

Takis appeared. Thin, medium height, greying hair spiked with gel, small dark eyes, and an earring in his left ear. Close up he seemed much older than the photos all over the media. His timing was so perfect I assumed he'd been eavesdropping, but one glance was enough to disprove that: apart from a glittering tiara he was stark naked and seemed to be spaced out of his mind. "Baby! Where you been all this time? I'm waiting for you!"

Vanessa looked uneasy. This obviously wasn't what she'd planned. "Takis, I'm talking to Mr Louridis, who's the manager of..."

"Baby, I told you, I'm waiting. I want you *now*. Tell the jerk to phone later."

It took him a few seconds to focus his eyes and realize that I was actually there.

"You're Loumidis?"

"Louridis."

"Whatever. What do you want?"

"To talk about some beautiful memories."

I stepped up close to him and took out the photo that Peppas had given me. Comparing it with the naked man in front of me I saw that his belly had got much smaller. It wasn't his only small anatomical feature.

"What are you talking about? What's this?" Vanessa demanded, trying to see the photograph.

The brain can do amazing things. Takis' seemed to clear as soon as he saw the photograph. He'd sobered up enough to hide it behind his back, tell his girlfriend not to stick her nose in and send her off so that we could be alone.

"But where can I go?" she asked plaintively.

"Anywhere you like. Have a massage or something. Off you go!"

She left, slamming the door as hard as she could. Takis didn't even wince. He sat down in the rocking chair and was looking at the photograph. He was still wearing the tiara.

"Whose manager did you say you were?" he asked.

"My own."

There was no reason to keep up the charade.

"Of course. And the only person who could have given you this is Hermes Peppas. Strange. I don't remember it being taken. Maybe I had popped one too many that evening. The question is, why Hermes gave it to you. I thought we were friends – unless you stole it."

"It doesn't matter who gave it to me or why."

"Right. If these things don't matter to you, let's talk about something that does. Like how much you're asking for it. This and any copies you've made. And whether you can persuade me that you haven't scanned and stored it electronically, because otherwise you're not getting a cent out of me. Start with how much."

"I don't want money."

"I'll bet," he sniggered.

I stared at him.

"I don't want money," I repeated.

The second time I was perhaps more convincing, because he fell quiet for a while, his eyes fixed on me.

"What *do* you want?"

"Information."

"What kind of information?"

"About Aliki Stylianou's disappearance. And anything you can say to help me find out where she is."

"What makes you think I know any more than Hermes?"

"I'm asking if you do."

"What if I don't?"

"I want you to try and remember. From what I've been told you and Aliki were together for some time."

"We were never seen in public. We never appeared together, we just fucked. I'm going to have a drink, what about you?"

"No."

"Your loss. We've got everything here. *Everything.*"

He got up shakily, leaving the tiara on the coffee table, went to the fridge and took out a bottle of tequila. Slumping down in the chair he opened it and took a swig, spilling half of it over his naked body.

"Oh, fuck! And Vanessa isn't here to lick it off!"

He began to laugh at his own joke. A real gentleman, the kind every girl dreams of. Or what every advisor puts up with: a prick with the white powder.

"What kind of information do you want?"

"Let's start with an easy question. Do you know any of these guys?"

I had the photos of Makis and Linesman ready on my phone.

"Never seen them before. This one looks like one of those neo-Nazi fruits," he said, pointing at Linesman.

Coked out, but spot on.

"What about Elsa Dalla?"

"Never met her, never heard her name until she was killed."

"Vassilis Stathopoulos?"

"Only seen him on TV. Poor sap. Hump her, yes, oh, yes. But marry her? Come on!" he sneered.

"Moving on to any little detail you can remember: did she have a relationship once that left its mark? Someone who threatened her, someone she was afraid of? From what I've learnt she seems to be a girl of many secrets."

"You watch too many films, pal."

Well, that was true.

"You make her sound like some femme fatale. She's just a little slut, a beautiful little slut, of course, who doesn't hesitate to screw anyone she needs to further her career."

He waved the photograph to emphasize his point. And he took another swig from the bottle, which he spilt as before. "If these girls weren't so deluded how would we get the chance to screw them, eh? Everything turns out for the best in this life. Here's to false impressions!"

He laughed and drank again.

I remembered what Lena Hnara had said about Aliki: *All her exes worship her. Even today. She keeps in touch with them all and no one's ever said a mean word against her.*

I wondered if there was anyone in this case who really knew anything about the people around them.

"Think a bit more," I insisted.

"Otherwise, what? I still don't understand. If I don't tell you something that's worth your while coming here, what are you going to do? Send the photograph to the press, to create a fuss now that Aliki has disappeared?"

"No, and I don't have any other copies."

He stared at me, trying to work out if I was having him on.

"Who's got them?"

"The guy who gave me the photograph."

"Are you… collaborating with him?"

"No. He's doing me a favour."

Vrettos took the photograph and looked at it, smiling. Then he tore it into two, four, eight pieces.

"If our friend has a copy, then only he can threaten me. You got nothing to offer me. Show me another one of these and maybe then I'll try to remember something."

"You don't understand… I'm not threatening you with the photo."

"But?"

Two quick steps and a reasonably strong – I thought – punch. Maybe a tad stronger than I'd intended, because I knocked him out of the armchair, which rocked for a while. He tried to get up, but was too dizzy. He stayed down.

"You crazy? Do you know who I am? I'll have your arse for break…"

"… fast", he wanted to say, but before he finished I kicked him towards the balcony door, which was tinted with a few weak sunbeams. "I know something better. I know *what* you are. You're somebody who's alive, but only for now," I said.

To make my point I picked him up and threw him back into the rocking chair. He hit it with such force he nearly turned it over.

"What you have to understand is that I'm here on a friendly visit. I'm trying to find and help a girl with whom you've shared some precious moments. I believe she's in danger, which is why we don't have time to waste. You're going to have to help me *now*, Takis, my friend."

He moaned, then coughed, spat out a tooth and looked at it in his hand, in disbelief. He wiped the blood from his upper lip.

"Le… let me think," he said, his voice shaking.

He was smart enough to understand he should really be afraid. And for types like him, the fear of getting hurt was perhaps the greatest of all. Like Al Goddard, the character played by Alan Ladd in 1951's *Appointment with Danger*, a film with so many great lines I never tire of seeing it. Goddard is speaking to Joe Regas, who tells him: "You look like you just lost your best friend." Al replies: "I *am* my best friend." And Regas says, "That's what I said." Takis Vrettos loved only himself and trembled for fear that something nasty might happen to his beloved.

"I'm waiting," I said. Then it all came rushing out.

"Not much impressed me… apart from her body… Even a blind man – if he touched her – would see light… She thought she was very talented… she would do anything…

to succeed... as an actress... modelling wasn't... wasn't good enough. All young broads in sh... show business are willing... I've met many... But few of them have that craziness in their eyes when they tell you about their plans... as if they are ready to swallow whoever gets in their way... Can I have a drink?"

He pointed to the tequila. I nodded.

"So, Aliki had the craziness?"

"Oh, yes. *Oh, yeah.* But she didn't show it to the world. When we were on our own and had drunk too much she would change completely... Lioness... she said she could tell me anything because I shared her craze... craziness to be number one... that's why she was with me... she believed I was on the same track."

"Weren't you?"

"Depends how you look at it. From what I hear on TV she's disappeared and might be dead. I'm shut up in this place until I persuade the bank's board of directors that I'm clean..."

He smiled weakly, spitting out blood.

"Craziness aside, anything else about Aliki?" I asked.

He bent his head, trying to remember. "Apart from the craze... nothing. She never talked to me about her past. She only spoke about the future: what she would do, how she would succeed, how I could help her become a household name... I didn't tell her anything about my past, either. No reason. None of us cared enough. We were living the moment."

"But sometimes you weren't living it alone."

"What do you mean?"

"That you sometimes had company. And you made videos."

He wasn't expecting that. "That's something you didn't get from Hermes."

If he expected me to reply, he was disappointed.

"Generally, I don't say no – you've seen that from the photo. It's even better when I get two women in bed with me. Who doesn't enjoy that? But we didn't do it very often during the six months Aliki and I spent together, we didn't want everyone hearing about it. So we kept it down to once or twice a month, with some eager little fan of Aliki's or a chick I might be dating at the time."

"How old were the fans?"

"What?"

"You said 'little fan'. How old were they?"

"Didn't ask them for ID."

"Were they underage?"

"That's relative."

"They were either over or under eighteen."

"Over fifteen a girl's a woman."

The co-star of the video was underage. Aliki had forgotten to mention that.

"That's what you say. Some paedophiles say 'over twelve', others 'over ten'. Once you're on that road you make up the rules to suit yourself."

"I thought you came to find information about Aliki, not to make moral judgements."

"I don't care what you thought," I told him.

"Are you here to kill me?" he asked.

"You're not important enough. Have you ever been with the same fan twice?"

"No."

"And how many of those occasions did you film?"

"Every time."

"Did the girls know?"

"No."

"Could they have found out about it later?"

I felt tired even asking him about this. Another angle to the case? Someone wanting revenge for being exploited? Or maybe someone close to the exploited girls? There could be scores of suspects.

"We didn't circulate the videos, they were just for us."

"And the copies are...?"

"In my cabinet. Except one I gave as a separation present to Aliki."

"A separation present?"

"Yes. She'd met Stathopoulos. Bigger fish than me, and he seemed to be really interested in her. She came, we talked, she explained, we drank, we did a couple of lines and she left, with my best wishes."

"And the video as a present."

"Yes."

Takis, the big-hearted.

"She did say something strange that evening, before she left. But she was so high by then, I didn't pay much attention."

"What was it?"

"She said that she really liked me because I never forced her to do anything. That I was almost as good-looking as the one man in the world she wanted to have amazingly beautiful children with. And when I asked her who this lucky guy was, she blushed and giggled and said it was her brother."

"Aliki hasn't got a brother; she's an only child."

"That's what I thought, and that's what she'd told me, but when I asked her that evening she went all giggly and said something like 'You don't know everything', so I just assumed she was making things up."

"The video – weren't you afraid that someone like her, who wants publicity, might do you harm?"

"Harm me? No chance. *She's in it.* And she wants to become a serious actress; she'd never release her own sex video to the press. And, at the end of the day, what my clients are after is money. As long as they keep making fortunes, they could hear that I killed my mother in cold blood and still no one, *no one* would leave Omikron."

His head suddenly flopped onto his chest. "I don't know anything else. You'll just have to believe me. Please," he said.

He was trembling. I told him that I believed him. I also told him that we had one more little problem. The problem was that I couldn't trust him not to phone security the moment I left. He could phone the police later, of course but, with the amount of drugs in his room, he would probably refrain. Especially since he didn't know who I was, and the most he could charge me with was beating him up a little. I explained that if I had to pay a return visit, I wouldn't stop at beating him up. Of course he assured me that he wouldn't go to the police and wouldn't even think of phoning down to reception. And of course I didn't believe him.

I told him that the solution was simple. I would give him a tap on the head that would knock him out for ten minutes or so. By the time Vanessa returned I'd be long gone. Takis wasn't that keen on the idea, but then he considered the alternatives and led me into his bedroom. "This OK?" he asked, turning his back.

"Fine," I told him.

"I'm a bit nervous. Like at one of those water parks, when you're at the top of the…"

"Slides," he was going to say, before he collapsed onto the bed.

36

It had been ten years since I last visited Patras. That was on business too. I had been hired by a very rich and very old lady who didn't at all like the way dozens of animals were being killed in her neighbourhood. I was just twenty five and had to accept some jobs that didn't entirely meet my standards, making concessions, as we all do, in the hope that sometime we will reach the point where we're our own master. I visited the lady in her country house, in the Rio suburb, where she had created a shelter to house about twenty cats, thirty dogs, five hares and a twittering of parrots and canaries. Her snow-white hair was like a wind-blown bird's nest and her expensive clothes were in odd contrast with her long, dirty nails and the hairs that bristled on her chin. She seemed completely cracked but had money to spend, so I wasn't bothered either by her crankiness or by the job she wanted me to do. She showed me photographs. Cats shot in the head. Dogs tied up and burnt alive, butchered or hung in trees, or all of them together. Suddenly she seemed a lot less crazy. She didn't know who was responsible for what she showed me. She wanted me to find him and take care of him. I explained that usually my employer knows the target and leaves me to get on with it; that detective work was extra, and would cost her considerably more. She opened up the huge suitcase she had by her side. It was stuffed full of twenty-euro notes. She said that she didn't know how much was in there but that I could have it all. As long as I accepted the job.

It took me two weeks to find him, but find him I did. I caught him red-handed and it wasn't difficult to get him to confess that it was he who had tortured all the other animals as well. Mid-thirties, no friends or family, working at home writing software. The walls of his room filled with photos of dead animals. Usually that type of person turns into a serial killer of people but he had taken a different direction. He told me that he'd give me a lot of money if I let him go. I explained how much I was getting paid. "For that kind of money, I'd kill me too", he'd said, and tried to grab a knife from a drawer. Contrary to popular belief, human life is often greatly overrated.

They found him after a few days, because of the stink coming from the rubbish bin. I didn't expect them to find him, but the refuse collectors went on strike and he was stuck there for days. The old lady was so pleased with my choice of his penultimate resting place that she doled out another bunch of notes.

Patras had only minimally changed since then. When I'd visited it last, its downward spiral had already begun. A city that lives off industry can't easily learn to exist without it. The first wave of poverty resulting from the deindustrialization of the city was halted for a while in the usual Greek way, by the rural unemployed moving to Athens. The opening of the country's borders, however, brought to Patras, as to much of Greece, a wave of Balkan immigrants who replaced the local poor. And now, with the newer wave of refugees from Africa trying to reach Patras in the hope of getting onto a ship leaving for Italy, things were going from awful to appalling. If there hadn't been tens of thousands of students there, supporting the local economy, Patras would have been a dead city, without hope of resurrection.

As I found out, it still kept the old custom of non-cooperation between the municipal and state services. In Patras, if the electricity, phone, water or any other organization wanted to dig up the road to repair or upgrade their networks, they didn't feel any obligation to inform the others. The same road is dug up again and again for months every year, creating a permanent traffic problem, which often makes Athens look comparatively efficient. A problem that I was reintroduced to when I arrived after two hours on the motorway, bound for the refugee area south-east of the city.

The area didn't get its name from the more recent wave of refugees, but back in 1922, when thousands of Greek refugees arrived in Patras from Asia Minor. At the beginning they found shelter wherever they could, in schools and warehouses, and then built their first houses. Illegal, of course, and outside the city plan, like at least half of the houses in Patras. All the new houses were two-storey dwellings, more-or-less identical, with one or two rooms per family, a yard shared by the whole block and a shared coffin, which after each funeral was returned to the church for the next. Even at the end, the poor never really get their own space on this planet.

Maria had called on my mobile as I was driving towards Patras, to tell me that, after an exhaustive web search of old newspaper archives, she had found the website of a *Peloponnisos* collector. *Peloponnisos* is the oldest newspaper printed in Patras and this guy had scanned and posted on the web every single page of every single issue of the newspaper from the past fifty years. In a two-column article, the day after Aliki's parents had their fatal car accident, Maria read that all possibilities, including that of a criminal act, which the police had found reasons to suspect, were being investigated. But in the next issues of the paper no further mention was made of the case. As soon as Maria had finished, Drag called, not with news about Aliki or Vassilis but about Nikos Zois' factory – after all the praise I'd heard about him from Teri, I'd asked Drag to check him out, and it seemed that the factory was doing so badly it was one step away from bankruptcy. We would have to inform the love-struck Teri that her lover wasn't exactly thriving in the way he'd told her.

There are women whose wrinkles enhance their looks. Not many, which is why the way they conquer time is so striking. Usually these women weren't beauties in their youth. Their lives beautified them. Just try to explain that to the hordes of middle-aged women who crowd the offices of plastic surgeons.

Roula Siouti was still beautiful. She lived in a street of houses without numbers, which didn't exactly help me to find her little two-storey house with the tiny garden that she had described to me on the phone. All the houses were similar constructions of stone and reinforced concrete, with roofs that seemed to have been thrown on any old how – remains of the refugee dwellings of the thirties. Today most of the people living there are foreigners who manage to cram their large families into one or two rooms. The houses in the street looked so alike that I had to stop and ask a group of kids playing football, who showed it to me.

Roula lived alone on the bottom floor. On the doorbell was written "Siouti", her married name. This wasn't however the name that interested me but her family name, Nikolidaga. She was Aliki Stylianou's aunt, her father's only sister. After a lot of phoning around people with the same surname, I got through to a cousin of hers with whom she kept in contact.

On the phone she had seemed calm. As if she were expecting the call, unwelcome though it was. I had introduced myself as Labis Louridis, private detective. I find it easy to change my supposed profession, depending on who I'm talking to, but I try to restrict the number of names I use in any one case, so that I don't get confused when I'm addressed by them. She had told me that she'd cut off relations with Zachos, her brother, quite some time before his death and she hadn't seen Aliki for years. I'd replied that it was her family's past I was interested in. When I asked her how many children her brother had and she asked me why I wanted to know, I knew straight away that something was up. Nobody answers one question with another if they have nothing to hide "Didn't Aliki have a brother?" I asked, to show her I knew what I was talking about – even if I didn't.

"What a can of worms you're stirring up now. Better let it rest," she said. I didn't ask her anything else on the phone. I pressured her to let me visit, saying that it would be better for her to talk to someone who wasn't a cop, that I would be completely discreet, that I was a friend of Aliki's from another case I'd helped her with and I believed she was alive and in hiding and I wanted to help her out. It took time to persuade her but my bluff of going to the police worked. According to one of the surveys that Teri is always reading, an overwhelming majority of people, when asked, say that they would do anything to avoid making a statement at a police station.

"How much do you know about Thanos?" she asked me, after we sat down on the sofa and she offered me the baklava she had just prepared.

"Not as much as I would like," I told her.

Her home was very simply furnished, and what furniture there was in that matchbox of a living room was old but well-preserved. She lived entirely off the alimony paid by her ex-husband. In the corners there were all kinds of children's toys: balls, dolls, board games.

Seeing my interest she explained, a fond smile on her lips: "The neighbourhood kids… they come here, play hide-and-seek, leave their stuff all over the place. Some of them have parents who work all day, or maybe they're not yet fluent in Greek, so I help them with their lessons. I never managed to become a mother so I try to be good auntie Roula."

Her eyes reminded me of something… maybe a tired version of Aliki's, when she'd said "to our health" in La Luna, right after "he'd thrash me once again". I wasn't sure. For the most part Roula didn't look like her niece at all. Maybe I'd seen those eyes and that smile somewhere else.

"Tell me about Thanos," I said.

"A very intelligent child. Really, extremely intelligent. His teachers all said the same. Even Zachos, my brother, seemed to soften when he talked about him. And Zachos almost never allowed himself to soften; he was a very hard man... unbelievably hard with everyone except Thanos. He had those under him in the army trembling... I don't know how he turned out like that. Our parents... they were the sweetest people you'd ever meet. Zachos had no respect for them, he considered them weak. If you didn't have connections in the right places my brother wouldn't give you the time of day. He left home at eighteen, never came back to see them. He didn't even go to their funeral – he was stationed in Evros, at the border, and sent me a letter saying that he couldn't ask for leave because he'd just been promoted. I should have cut him out of my life then, as I threatened, but I always had such a weakness for him... It seemed that the harsher his behaviour towards us was, the more I felt I had to be there for him, in case he needed me. By the time he returned to Patras, many years later, he was a brigadier, the youngest in the army, as he kept telling everyone. He was very proud of himself. He had connections with both the main political parties. Members of parliament and ministers were always ringing him up. He believed that it wouldn't be long before they'd appoint him as head of the army, at least, maybe of all the armed forces. But then the whole thing with Thanos blew up."

She stopped and sipped some tea.

"Thanos was Zachos' pride and joy. Aliki did well at school and was very pretty, like her mother, but Zachos regarded women as purely decorative. He didn't have to say it; you could see it in the way he behaved. He wanted his wife and daughter to shine on every public occasion, but that was it. If either of them dared to open their mouths and he didn't like what they said, he'd humiliate them."

Exactly the way of behaving that Lena Hnara had attributed to Vassilis. Had Aliki set out to find a man who was exactly like her father?

"While Thanos… Whatever he said, from the time when he could only babble, his father listened to it like a papal pronouncement. He adored, he simply adored him. Until the day he came home and found Thanos in bed with a boy, one of his classmates. He beat both of them and threw Thanos out of the house. Without clothes, money, anything… A boy of just sixteen – out on the streets. Worse than what he had done to our parents."

She halted, tears in her eyes, and put her hand over her mouth to stop herself from sobbing.

"And… his wife?"

"Pleaded with him frantically, night and day. To no effect. So she set out on her own to find Thanos, without results. Someone told her he'd seen her son catch the bus to Athens, but that was it. She kept up the search for years. On the rare occasions we met she told me that some detectives had raised her hopes but ended up cheating her, and she had to hide her efforts from Zachos, who had forbidden her even to mention his son's name again. She began to take pills, then to spend periods in the psychiatric hospital… God help me for what I'm going to say, but dying in that accident was a release for her. And as for Zachos… When he threw Thanos out, he lost the last of his humanity. He had nothing to give or get from anyone. Only military decorations."

"Are you sure it was an accident?"

It was as if I had suddenly slapped her.

"What… what do you mean… the police had investigated… an accident, for sure, they'd assured me…"

"So, nobody knows where Thanos is."

"Nobody cares enough to find out any more. Not even me. I wish him well, but…"

But I've had enough pain in my life without going searching for more, she meant but didn't say.

"And Aliki? What was her relationship with Thanos?" I asked.

"Good, I think. Very good. I didn't see them very often, though… I told you… my brother didn't think I was important enough to get close to. But they seemed to love each other."

"Didn't she stand up to her father when he chucked him out?"

"There are people you simply can't stand up to. I guess it was also the shock – all that coming out of the blue. I can't remember how she reacted. She was always locked up in herself, a very quiet child. I think that she just accepted it. What else could she do? She was very young then, only eleven, still at junior school."

A long silence followed. Grief had enfolded her, isolating her from her surroundings. I coughed, just to let her know I was still there, thanked her for the information and asked her to show me some photographs of Aliki's family. She picked up an album from a shelf on the little table on which she had put our drinks.

"I keep them here," she said, with a smile that for a moment seemed to forgive everything at the sight of those she had learnt to call "her own", even if they weren't.

I took the album from her hands and looked at the photograph. "1994" was written under it. I saw a smiling Aliki, her father, mother and her brother. I saw them and the biggest shiver I had ever felt shook my whole body.

"Are you alright?" Roula asked.

She must have seen the blood leave my face. I think that I managed to thank her as I rushed out of the house and ran to my car, as fast as my legs could carry me.

37

Ten years later, in the same city, and yet again just a photograph was enough to completely change my view. Then it was of dead animals. Now it was of a man who had died but had been resurrected. A very dangerous man, who was officially missing. A man like me.

I now had almost the whole picture of what had happened. Something had gone wrong many, many years ago. And now nobody could put it right. I could only do my best to rescue the innocent. I drove like a maniac down the motorway, with my foot flat to the floor – other drivers pulling their cars over to avoid me, sounding their horns in alarm and anger. I called Drag again and again. He had chosen the worst time not to pick up.

The only thing I couldn't work out was the motive. Not for the killings. For getting me involved in the case. I racked my brains without getting anywhere as the car rattled over potholes. Could they have picked me at random? Maybe they were just looking for someone in my field of work and stumbled across me? It wasn't improbable, but luck is always low on my list of possible explanations. I was at the toll collection booth, eighteen miles outside of Athens, when I got an idea. A far-fetched idea, given the long list of people I had confronted in my life – whoever was after me could have been connected with any number of my old cases. I called Angelino and told him it was a matter of life and death. He called back in twenty minutes, confirming what I feared.

An hour and a half later, I was outside Teri's house. She hadn't answered the telephone either. Nor had Maria. All kinds of nightmarish scenarios had passed through my mind as the Peugeot ticked off the miles. You spend all your life training yourself to keep cool in the most difficult situations then you discover how inadequate your training was.

I drove up to the house at normal speed so as not to arouse suspicion. The windows and the curtains were shut, and out in the road Drag's Nissan was parked. My mobile rang. I saw Drag's name on the screen and picked it up with relief.

"Where are you?" I asked.

"He's right here, with your friends Teri and Maria. Get out of the car without hanging up. You've got thirty seconds to reach the front door, or you'll listen to them die."

It was Aliki.

38

Anything is allowed in dreams. Faces and bodies blend in improbable ways, sometimes disgusting you and sometimes making you frustrated that you woke up before the dream was over.

I opened my eyes to see Aliki kissing someone whose face looked a lot like hers, but who had the muscular body of a man. Nikos Zois lifted her effortlessly from the floor, while greedily kissing her, his tongue in her mouth.

I didn't know how much time had passed since I'd run to the entrance of Teri's house to find Maria, Drag and Teri handcuffed to chairs and Aliki holding a gun to their heads. She'd ordered me to drop my gun and Zois had knocked me out with a blow to the back of the head.

Now all four of us were sitting in Teri's living room, with our hands cuffed behind our backs. Drag seemed to be in a bad state, with blood on his face. Not, however, as bad as the savagely beaten and unconscious Vassilis Stathopoulos, who was bound hand and foot on the floor.

I blinked, but it wasn't a dream.

They had turned now and were smiling at me. Aliki and Zois. The siblings from hell. As I was driving like a maniac on the motorway, I had figured out that they were accomplices. But I never imagined they were lovers.

"Hello, Aliki. Hello, Thanos," I said, trying to contain the buzzing in my head.

Zois and Aliki exchanged looks. Aliki seemed uneasy, he merely smiled.

"Very impressive!" he sneered.

"I do my best."

"What else do you know?"

In such situations, it's a good idea to play for time, in case help arrives. Except we couldn't expect help from anywhere. Our only hope was that our captors might momentarily lose focus and give us a chance to act. Though what action we could take against two armed lovers who'd handcuffed us to chairs was another question.

"I know the basic facts. About your father, about how much you and he loved each other, about murdering your parents and making it seem like an accident…"

"Our poor old mum and dad… Such a shame…"

They laughed. Both him and Aliki. In a macabre way that made Aliki, in particular, seem transformed, her beauty distorted by the veil of madness I was seeing for the first time.

"Is that all you know? Nothing else about Daddy?"

"I know that he threw you out of the house when he caught you buggering a boy. But seeing the two of you now, I think he found you with Aliki."

"Excellent! Who have you been talking to, my aunt in Patras? Roula has a big mouth. I should have shut it, really, but I couldn't be bothered – she knows so little of the truth that it's not worth it. Well done, though. I thought you were much dumber. Well done."

He had got close to me as he was talking and he suddenly pistol-whipped me across my face. Maria let out a cry and

Teri said something – probably a curse – that I couldn't understand. Sometimes pain overwhelms you, but though I felt as if my head was ready to detach from my neck, this wasn't one of the times when I could let the pain win. I closed my eyes, trying once more to rein it in. I failed. When I opened them again, Zois had walked round my chair and approached his sister. He grabbed her by the waist and kissed her again. Aliki pressed herself to him, returning the kiss with the same fervour. I noticed that both their guns had silencers.

If looks could kill, Teri would have made Zois evaporate. Maria was looking down, as if lost in thought. I had warned her, when she had allowed me to live in her house, that sometime violence could come knocking on our door. "We'll throw it out together," she'd responded. I don't know if she'd been fully aware of what she was saying; if she'd really believed that she would ever go through an experience like this.

"So, this was to take your revenge on your father? Sleeping with Aliki?" I asked Zois.

Aliki smiled at the question. A demented, twisted smile so how could it still appear so radiant? She looked at her brother. He nodded.

"I don't blame you. Most little people, like you, can't understand," she said. "This has nothing to do with revenge. Revenge is complicated. Revenge is dirty. This... this I pure," she said, looking at him with adoration.

"Pure incest. There's a new one," Drag said.

"Pure *love*. Purer than any other kind," Zois almost shouted. "People spend their whole lives trying to under-stand their spouses, because they don't *know* them, and they never will. No one really ever knows who you are, except the person you grew up with. Only she knows and loves you for life."

"That's your proposal? That we all go fuck our brothers and sisters?" Teri said.

"I understand fucking is the only thing you know, freak, but it is irrelevant here. This is love, it has no other name. Incest is what *he* did to her."

"*Freak*", he had called her. She'd fallen head over heels for his act, and now she had to listen to this.

"Your father?" I asked Zois, trying not to think how Teri must have been feeling.

"Daddy," Aliki said.

"Aliki developed very early. When she was ten years old, the first one to notice and take an interest was the brigadier," Zois said.

"So very pleased that I was acquiring the body of a woman."

"Every evening – every evening he would go to her bed to stroke and caress her."

"Then he'd get me to caress him. First through his pyjamas, then inside them. His back, his chest, then down and down. And I didn't mind. I didn't mind at all what I learnt. I *wanted* to learn, however disgusted I was by my teacher. I asked him to show me more, so that I could learn to satisfy him completely. So that I could put into practice what I had learnt with the man I truly loved."

She stood on tiptoe and licked Zois' cheek. If love and showing off were connected, those two were very much in love.

"Until, one day, dear Daddy came in and caught us

making love. He went bananas," Zois said, enjoying the feeling of her tongue.

"After beating up Thanos he said that he would kill him if he found him anywhere near me again."

"To be exact, what he said was: 'You fucking pervert, I'll cut you into pieces if you lay your hands on her again.' He knew I liked boys, he didn't approve but basically he didn't care. What he wanted was exclusive rights to Aliki. The same man that I used to worship when I was a kid," chuckled "Zois" – I still thought of him by that name.

"Well, aren't all good daddies demanding?" said Aliki.

"Next time he found us together he threw me out of the house, supposedly to stop me from smearing the family name because I was a gay pervert. He even got one of his connections in the registry office to delete any record of my birth. He wanted to wipe me out, erase all evidence I'd ever existed."

"And your mother did nothing," I said to Aliki who, despite everything, seemed to be slightly more human than her brother. I don't know why; maybe the fact that she looked like an angel and acted like a devil created a picture, the shadows needing the light to emerge. Or, maybe, looking into her blue eyes I saw not what she was but what she might have been.

"Took a couple of pills and slept through to the following morning. That's the way Mummy tackled all her problems."

As Aliki was talking, I noticed that Vassilis was the only one of us who was tied with rope rather than handcuffs. And, in spite of the mess he was in, he was trying, as unobtrusively as he could, to untie his bonds. I didn't know what he could do if he managed it, but there was hope – the strength of despair always carries surprises. I had to continue to divert their attention as best as I could. Aliki and Zois held all four of us hostage. They held my whole life hostage. As Reno Smith says in *Bad Day at Black Rock*, "I believe that a man is as big as what'll make him mad." The idea that something might happen to Drag, Maria and Teri was what made me mad. The only difference was that, unlike in film noir, we couldn't afford any losses.

Teri spoke before I did.

"Yeah, stick with each other. You're a great couple. You'll have great babies, too!" she said.

"Shut up, freak!" Aliki shouted, slapping her.

And I thought she seemed slightly more human.

When Teri raised her head again, she was ready. She spat with the accuracy that was well known to us and got Aliki right in the eye. My friend may have changed gender, but still had some of her manly skills. In reply, Zois gave her a punch that jolted her back in her chair, which crashed to the ground. Teri lay still, unconscious.

"Dirty whore," he said.

Maria, next to me, started to sob uncontrollably. The look in Zois' eyes told me he was ready to kill us, and although Drag was on the verge of eruption, there really was nothing we could do. Yet. I spoke quickly, keeping a check on Vassilis out of the corner of my eye, hoping that he was getting somewhere.

"I have a couple of questions that confuse me," I said to Zois.

"Don't strain yourself. For a man with your IQ, you've done brilliantly," he replied.

His anger had now turned into a smile, his face glowing with paranoia. When I first saw his smile I'd thought that it was familiar, but I'd never realized it was a carbon copy of Aliki's. I noticed his eyes; the same as his aunt's and yet so different. It was only when I saw the photograph of him as a child that I understood what Roula Siouti's eyes reminded me of. So many similarities that took me too long to see. I had to keep talking.

"Elsa had a fixation on you," I said to Aliki. "She wanted more than anything to look like you, that's why she kept on with the plastic surgery. So you took advantage of it. You gave her the car from time to time, so you could escape your husband's surveillance. With a wig and the same clothes, from a distance you looked the same. Every now and then she played you while you and Thanos arranged your plan."

"In dim light no one could tell us apart, even if they were close. No one. Not even my dear husband. He came home plastered after a reception one night, and I got Elsa to join him in bed. She talked to him in the dark, mounted him and he couldn't tell there was any difference at all… Elsa loved it. The sense of danger, the chance to play me… She thought it was also great practice for her acting… 'How many people get the chance to play a role like this in their daily lives?' she used to say."

"Role-playing is what most people do," I said.

"When you have such a woman… *any* woman, and you can't tell the difference between her and another, drunk or sober, night or day, then you don't deserve her," Zois said, looking at Vassilis.

He might have been crazy, but he sometimes made sense.

"That was the night you took the black and white photo you have in your living room," I said.

Something had seemed strange about it from the beginning, something that I couldn't pinpoint till I managed to fit together all the pieces. It was her fingers: those long, slender fingers that had caught my attention in La Luna had been replaced by Elsa's much stubbier ones in the photograph.

"Yes, Elsa took it, how did you know that?" Aliki said, smiling and showing the tip of her tongue.

"I'm psychic," I said.

If she was sick in the head then so was I, who could still be turned on by her, regardless of all she had done.

"How much did you promise her, apart from more sex?" I asked.

"Ten per cent, as soon as Vassilis was out of the way. But really, she would have done it all for less. Not for the sex; she wasn't very good at it and didn't enjoy it much. What she dreamt of was money and a career – I had promised she would play me in the TV series based on my life. Plus, she hated Vassilis. She'd thrown herself at his feet, back when they were a couple, asking him to forgive her, but he wouldn't hear of it. When he got the lowest scum let off lightly it didn't bother his conscience. It was being cuckolded that made him all moral and principled."

"Funny to hear you say the word 'scum' without looking in the mirror first," Drag told Aliki.

Once again, the right thing to say at the right time. Make them angry while we're still tied up. If anyone can aggravate me more than Drag, I'd like to meet him.

Zois smiled.

"You're not scared, eh?"

"Should I be?" Drag said.

"Don't worry. Before I'm finished with you you'll cower. Do you know how many shit themselves when the first bullet hits them? Lose control of their sphincter muscles… Incredible filth."

"Couldn't have described you better myself," Drag said.

Zois approached Drag and put his gun on Drag's forehead.

Maria and I exchanged glances. It was kind of romantic to die with my friends. But if we were eighty-five, not thirty-five. I played my last card.

"You know why they chose us?" I asked Drag.

Zois turned and looked at me. "You know that, as well? Please share."

"Stamatis Zafiriou," I said to Drag. "Better known to us as Linesman."

"My rival," Aliki said.

"I have his photo in my jacket pocket," I said quickly, trying to ride the wave of interest I'd caused. And to keep that gun away from Drag.

"What?" Zois said.

"Check my pocket."

He did. He got out the photo of Linesman, Elsa and Aliki at the bar and stared at his lover's face.

"Where did you get this?" Aliki said.

"It's on the web. You were with them that night, weren't you?" I said to Zois.

The slimeball who had taken the photograph would have done us a great favour if he had captured Zois with his lens in the first place, instead of just telling Drag that

Elsa and Aliki were all but fucking each other and the guy who was with them in that bar.

Zois was now caressing the photo.

"Stamatis," he murmured. "The only man I really loved. And you two…"

He was crying. Zois was actually trembling and crying. He had lowered his gun from Drag's forehead, but that didn't mean much. Maybe this was the moment he'd been waiting for. Maybe he would shoot us there and then, in an outburst of madness, spurred on by the memory of his lover and the sound of his name. Luckily, Aliki approached him from behind, kissed him on the back of the neck and embraced him. That seemed to calm him down, temporarily.

We hadn't paid attention when we'd heard that Linesman's lover was looking for us. And we hadn't given a thought to the possibility that his lover could be a "he". I made the connection when I found out about Zois' homosexuality and saw his photo in Roula's house, in Patras. Later, on the motorway, I called Angelino who confirmed in just a few minutes that Linesman was gay.

"You decided to kill two birds with one stone. Get me to take care of Vassilis and then kill us. Probably fix things to look like we're to blame for everything. I thought you said revenge is complicated and dirty," I told Aliki.

"Right. But oh so necessary, at times," she said. "They'll find a suitcase stuffed with money beside your bodies. Such disagreements are common among scum like you."

Eyes that reminded me of the sea. The sea that drowns you.

"You know what a short memory this country has, Mr Dragas. All your successes will be discounted and you'll be dismissed as just another rotten cop, not worth remembering. That's the cherry on the cake. Stratos is a nobody. But you – we'll destroy your entire legacy," Zois said, in a matter-of-fact tone. He could have been describing how he took out the rubbish. Which, obviously, is how he thought of us.

I glanced at Vassilis, then quickly away again, so that I wouldn't draw attention to him. My eyes stopped at Maria's terrified look. If there was even the slightest chance to get her out of there alive…

I had to keep on talking.

"It was you who appeared on the set as her second bodyguard, a few times," I told Zois.

"Yeah, my baby needed to come and see me," Aliki replied on his behalf.

Aliki had blurted to Takis that he was almost as good-looking as her brother. And Sam had told me about the very good-looking second bodyguard. It had taken me too long to put these two facts together.

"And Elsa... you gave her the BMW, in one of your frequent switches and your brother murdered her in the middle of the street to cause a sensation. The more public the killing, the less suspicion is focused on you. If you wanted to kill Elsa, no one would have thought you'd do it in your own car in a public square."

"You can always count on the banality of people's assumptions," Zois said.

That was their tactic all along. To do the counter-intuitive thing. Make everybody certain that Aliki couldn't be behind it by the sheer extravagance of their actions. If she wanted to kidnap her husband and kill Makis, she surely wouldn't have done it so violently in her own home, leaving the door open for the police. Add to that the assassination attempts against her, and me telling Drag about the danger she was in from her husband... They had fooled us completely.

"Poor Elsa... She knew too much and we were tired of her hanging around. Getting rid of her was so easy it was pathetic... And she was pathetic in her loneliness. Apart from Regoudis, who had fallen for her – she only tolerated him to promote her career – there was absolutely nobody. Her family hated her; she had no friends," Aliki said.

"We did her a favour," Zois tittered. "She was actually happy, till she saw my gun – happy she had followed my instructions and got rid of Vassilis' surveillance guys."

"So everything made sense," Drag said. "It seemed like another attempt was being made to murder Aliki, your husband thought that you were scared and hiding because you didn't know who was hunting you, and we thought you were in hiding from your husband... And all the attempts against you, you faked from the start..."

"Thanos is a genius. Vassilis swallowed it completely, got worried and wanted to hire half the men in Athens as my bodyguards... No way he could make head or tail of what was happening..."

Vassilis, knowing they were talking about him, kept very still.

"But you, Stratos... You gave us a hard time," Aliki said.

"Sorry, I didn't mean to."

"I knew from Thanos all about you and your *research*, but you went overboard. You wanted to discover why exactly I wanted to kill him, and I had to persuade you how necessary it was… I can't think why a mere killer needs all these details."

Caretaker, I thought, but it wasn't the moment to correct her.

"But since you're so intent on ensuring your employer is acting from the right motives, we made sure you would be persuaded."

"And your friend, Lena? She doesn't have a clue, does she? You just used her friendship with Teri to approach me," I said to Allki.

"Lovely Lena… Stupid people are always so useful, don't you think? From the time I first kissed her, years ago, she became devoted to me forever, even if we didn't go to bed again. When we saw her talking with your pal, Teri… bingo! And she really believes that Vassilis attacked me, that he was behind the murder attempts! As if that dull creature would hit me or get Kristo, the Bulgarian, to intimidate me! He might humiliate me in public and be crazily jealous but if he'd have lifted a hand against me I'd have cut it off — or maybe fallen in love with him."

Drag turned towards me.

"I found Kristo's family and got them to give me Mr Zois' name – they said Kristo owed him big time. I came to tell Teri but Zois was already here. They gave me the same welcome they did you – with a gun pointed at the girls' heads."

"Not very heroic," I told Zois.

"Do you know many heroes who finally come out on top?" Zois asked.

249

"And all this for money. To be rich, together, with her husband's money, and maybe save your sinking factory," I said.

"Times are tough, the country is going bankrupt, everybody wants to flee abroad... If you don't have a rich benefactor or a big inheritance nowadays..." Zois said.

"Rich is good. But the '*together*' is what truly matters," Aliki said, her eyes shining as the words left her lips.

I wondered if she could see how different their responses were. I wondered if she ever thought about why he left her with their parents and disappeared for years, if he loved her so much. That might be a good inflammatory question, to gain us some more time. Or to make them finish us off immediately. I decided to say something else, hoping that Vassilis would soon make a move.

"Did you kill Antonis Rizos just to convince Lena that Vassilis was behind it all? To get her to testify that Vassilis killed him because he was jealous?"

"Partly, yes. But Thanos also wanted him dead because I'd fucked Antonis a couple of times. Purely out of charity: the poor man actually thought he was helping me get better! But my baby can be a little possessive at times," she said, obviously liking him that way. She gave him another long kiss.

"I want you to kill anybody who's ever fucked me," she said and kicked Vassilis in the ribs. Absolutely no reaction. He didn't even blink. His famous tenacity, the quality that had allowed him to win the most difficult cases, continued to give me hope.

"And at the fast-food joint? Why did you come to talk to me?" I asked Zois.

"Ah, that," he said, his smile widening. "That was one of my favourite moments. You need to have some fun from time to time. And to meet your adversaries up close. I saw you come back in and thought what a great opportunity to chat, with you having no idea what was going on! I almost had a hard-on, it was so exciting. Especially when I told you how I felt about your friend the freak."

He jerked his gun towards Teri. I was glad she was unconscious.

"You ate that stuff up. And it was so easy to say. I was really talking about how I feel for Aliki."

He could easily be lying again. Words had no weight for him, other than helping him achieve what he wanted.

"And you are an ignorant sociopath," he told me. It takes one to know one. "What makes you think you can decide who deserves to live and die? It's not as if you can distinguish the good from the bad."

"While you can?" I said.

"Of course. I distinguish the good of the others from what's good for me," he said.

"You and Aliki," I said.

"That's what he means," she said, quickly.

It was hardly the moment to feel sorry for her, but I did. Repeatedly raped by her father, she was clinging to her brother to survive. That was her life story. Only her brother was crazier than the brigadier.

"You can't have done it all by yourself. Especially Makis. Aliki must have come with you to their house, to keep the Rottweiler quiet," I told Zois.

"Of course," Aliki said. "With me by his side, there was no problem. And Makis came happily to meet me – he didn't even have time to realize that he was about to die," Aliki said.

"But why did you sleep with Makis? To make sure he'd kill Vassilis, if you failed to get me to do it?" I asked her.

"That's life. You have to fuck a few more people than you want to, to get what you need."

"Only he became too attached, looking for you desperately when you disappeared. And those crazy hieroglyphics were just another red herring to keep the cops busy," I said.

"Mmm… Of course, the hanging on the chandelier did seem a bit over the top. But what can I say; Thanos has his own peculiar sense of artistry, sometimes," said Aliki.

"Vassilis tried to escape, but didn't manage it. If he had it would have been the end for us," Zois said.

"But all's well that ends well," Aliki said.

"The end for you. A fresh start for us."

I noticed that Vassilis had managed to untie his right hand. I needed to keep them occupied for just a few more seconds. Our only chance. "You know what I think?" I said.

"Let *me* tell you what you're thinking," Zois answered. "You're thinking that now Vassilis has untied himself…"

He whipped round and shot Vassilis right in the chest. Maria screamed.

"… you would have had a chance to escape," he said.

Vassilis was still writhing on the ground, with Zois standing over him to finish him off, when all hell broke loose.

39

You never turn your back on someone who has nothing to lose.

This is what Zois did, to finish off Vassilis. And Drag, tied to the chair, attacked. With that head that can smash concrete, dragging his chair with him, he hit Zois right in the middle of his back.

Zois collapsed as if his legs had been cut from under him.

Aliki turned her gun on Drag, ready to fire. She didn't manage it.

I hurled myself and my chair at Aliki and managed to knock her off balance. Her bullet went wide and she dropped the gun. Zois was trying to retrieve his gun while I tried to kick Aliki's away. But before I got to it, a hand came up, holding the other gun.

"Is this… what you're looking for?" Vassilis said to Zois. And fired.

"I believe you. Thank you," Lena Hnara said to me when I phoned to tell her what had happened. I explained that everything Aliki had said to the psychiatrists had been true; all the cuts on her body she'd done herself. Right from her wedding day she had started to build her alibi. She'd told all the psychiatrists that she wanted to kill her husband during her bouts of madness, so that it wouldn't look pre-planned. The only therapist she'd told her made-up story about Vassilis torturing her was Rizos, the same story she told Lena, to convince her that Vassilis was the guilty party.

Lena thanked me, but there was no need. I had promised to tell her what I would find out. Life is a very simple affair, if you want it to be. You look after your own. You keep your promises. You do your job as well as you can. And, at the end of the day, you turn off the switch.

Of course, I only gave Lena the basics. There were many details that she didn't need to know. Like the fact that when Teri came to and we managed to untie ourselves, she stood over Zois' body and cried her heart out, saying again and again and again: "Worthless prick. I'd known from the beginning. I'd known from the beginning." Drag took her in his arms and held her until she stopped sobbing. I didn't tell Lena about the drawn-out howl that came from Aliki when she saw her brother dying from her husband's bullet. Or about the way she rushed towards her husband, her nails outstretched like talons, wailing like a banshee. The second and last of Vassilis' shots stopped her when she was right over him. They died at the same moment, their bodies entwined together for the last time. *I knew she was the one right from the beginning, since her first breath beside me. Have you ever been in love like that, Mr Gazis?*

Maria went and buried herself in Drag's arms, beside Teri, and they gestured for me to join them.

I put my arms round them.

Yes, I have been in love like that. With three people.

ACKNOWLEDGEMENTS

A huge thanks to Peter and Rosie Buckman, to whom I am more indebted than words can say.

Charles Pappas' book *It's a Bitter Little World* (Writer's Digest Books, 2005) was very helpful in double-checking certain movie lines in cases where my memory was reluctant to help.